A MEL DRED MYSTERY

THE ADVENTURE BEGINS

THREE GOLD COINS

TOO YOUNG TO DIE
THIS
RICH!

A MEL DRED MYSTERY
THE ADVENTURE BEGINS

THREE GOLD COINS
TOO YOUNG TO DIE
THIS
RICH!

John Kaufman

Three Gold Coins; Too Young to Die this Rich!

Printed in the United States of America
ISBN 978-1-64133-798-4 (sc)
ISBN 978-1-64133-799-1 (ebk)

2024.03.22

BlueInk Media Solutions
1111B S Governors Ave
STE 7582 Dover,
DE 19904

www.blueinkmediasolutions.com

TABLE OF CONTENTS

CHAPTER 1

Mildred Who? or Got a Rope?

Mel had been living with his father for most of his life. His mother had left when he was just a few years old. He did not miss her much. Mel and his dad had stopped being friends a long time ago. Mel had lived with his grandfather for the last few years, but his grandpa had become ill and passed away a few months ago, and now Mel was back living with his father.

Mel's father was the minister of the local Christian Revival Missionary Church. The only thing he asked of Mel was that Mel be in church every Sunday morning to hear his father lecture to each and every person in attendance, including his son, who seemed to have a mind of his own. His father used the word of God as an example to all whom he met, always preaching to others that only God has the answers to our prayers. Being a private investigator, Mel had long ago begun listening to the universe to hear the clues God was leaving for him to find. Mel, for now, figured that it did not hurt to have God on his side, clues or no clues!

It was a nice June day. Tomorrow, Mel had much to investigate; he had not been sleeping well at night. He kept trying to understand all the odd things his grandfather had muttered during his last few days alive. Again and again, Mel could hear his grandfather's words: "Nap, nap." Maybe he meant "map," not "nap." His grandfather kept grasping his hand and saying, "Well," and Mel kept replying, "No, Grandpa, you're not very well."

1

Suddenly Mel sat up in his bed. He realized there was a map of some sort in the old family well; that's what his grandfather had been trying to tell him. Tomorrow, bright and early, he would start investigating by visiting the old family well where his grandfather was born and raised. The land actually belonged to Mel now. The property had been left to him by his grandfather. It consisted of a couple of acres of trees and the old well, which was still standing by the little house. The house was in disrepair, but Mel and his grandfather had lived in it not so very long ago.

Mel was heading out the door by daybreak, dragging his backpack full of the things he might need. His motto was always "be prepared." He snuck out the front door, quietly closing the screen door behind him. Mounting his trusty iron steed, Mel headed down the road as fast as he could pedal. His father had brought him the bike, shortly after his grandfather had passed away. It was a road racer, and that's exactly what Mel was doing, racing down the road to find the secret hidden in the old family well.

It was not long before Mel was lowering himself down the well, careful not to lose hold of the rope that the water bucket was still connected to—or so he thought. Ohhhhhhhh! Plop! Mel was lying on his back but not in water. It was mud. His head was spinning, and his ears were ringing with what sounded very much like his grandfather's laughter! They had often laughed together while watching every *I Love Lucy* episode ever made on his grandfather's old black-and-white TV. Mel was in a daze from his unexpected fall. He quickly tried to clear his mind and come to his senses. Mel lay there in the gooey mire of sticky, wet mud, asking himself how he could have been so stupid. Tilting his head back, Mel could see the bright morning sky at the top of the well. He was lying in darkness, and he could not see, but it did not feel as if he had been hurt. Mel soon realized that the presence of the mud was most fortunate, as it had been a soft landing of sorts.

The first thought in Mel's mind was, *No one will ever find me here, and I'm surely doomed.* His mind was racing with thoughts of all the TV shows he had seen about people who were lost and never found. Mel lost all sense of composure and began screaming at the top of his lungs, "Help! Help! Someone please help me!"

Just when he had decided that yelling for help would be in vain, as no one could hear him back in town and he was surely doomed, Mel heard someone say, "Who's down there?"

Mel could not believe his ears. He yelled, "Mel, Mel Dread, Mel Dread!"

"Mildred, what are you doing down in that well?" Mel replied, "I am looking for friends."

"Friends? Why?" said the voice at the top of the well.

Mel could see a small face peering down the well from above. It took him a few seconds to realize she could not see him in the blackness at the bottom. Taking a deep breath, Mel answered as calmly as he could but rather loudly, "Because if you were my friend, you would lower the rope that you have up there down to me. In fact, that would be a very kind thing to do, friends or not! You see, I currently find myself in a severely disturbing predicament, so I am begging you to please kindly throw me a rope."

"Hey," Mel yelled as he felt the sting of a rope hitting him on he head. "Hey! Are you trying to kill me?" Mel could hear the stranger laughing.

"Without me, Mister, you might as well be dead," said the voice from above.

Covered with stinky, black-as-tar mud, Mel emerged from the well, smiling. "So, Missy, what brings you to this side of town?" "Well, first of all, I rode my bike. Second, my name is Bonnie, Bonnie Lou Starr. I am visiting my grandmother, who is Betty Jean Davidson. I am spending the summer with her. She lives across the street from you. I have tried my best to get you to notice me but in vain. You have ignored me." Bonnie would have kept right on talking if Mel had not interrupted her.

"Oh yeah," Mel responded, now vaguely remembering that in fact he had seen this new girl in church last Sunday. "How did you find me here, Miss Bonnie Lou Starr, if I may inquire?"

"Find you?" Bonnie laughed. "I have been following you for the past three days!"

Mel thought to himself that he needed to start paying more attention. He just smiled, shaking the mud off his pant legs. Then in his friendliest of voices, Mel said, "Nice to finally meet you, Bonnie Lou Starr. Mr. Mel Porter Dread at your service."

"Service? What the heck you talking about?" Bonnie asked. "What service?"

Mel winked at her and said in a deep, manly voice, "Melvin P. Dread, private investigator, solving any local mysteries and crimes, at your service."

Bonnie looked at Mel, who was covered with stinky well mud, and said, "What you need right now is a laundry service and a bar of Lava soap. After that, you need to tell me what you were doing stuck in the bottom of an old, abandoned well." Bonnie could be very persistent, and she was very smart. She already knew that Mel was not looking for friends, But she was sure that today was the day they both had found one, she thought.

Mounting their bikes, they headed toward home. Pulling into the yard, Bonnie yelled across the street, "Mel P. Dread, you must never forget I saved your life!"

Mel yelled, "Thanks again." He knew how fortunate meeting little Bonnie Starr had been for him. She had saved Mel's life, and he knew they would be friends forever. Forever is a very long time for two adventuresome kids growing up in the Midwest!

It was about 6:00 p.m., and Mel could see Bonnie sitting on her front porch across the street. He politely asked his father if he could be excused from the dinner table as he wanted to spend some time outside before the sun went down. His father nodded and went back to reading his Bible, which he did every night after dinner, sometimes for hours. "Well, I have been waiting for you, Mel," little Bonnie said with anticipation in her voice. She was ready to ask her newfound friend a million and one questions, and without any hesitation, she began with,

"How old are you, Mister?"

"I will soon celebrate my twelfth birthday. What else can I tell you besides that I am smart as a cookie, I am sharp as a sword, and I am wiser than most men twice my age—also, I am not the kind of guy who likes to brag about himself. Besides, I plan to find a hidden treasure, sooner rather than later, which will make me rich beyond my wildest dreams." Mel spoke as if he knew something and little Bonnie Starr did not.

Bonnie was eager to find out what that was, and she knew how. "Okay, Mel P. Dread, this is how I see it. If it were not for me, you would still be at the bottom of that old well. Mel, honestly, why were you down in that well? Mel, I saved your life and you must tell me! Why you were down in that old well? For the last time, tell me!"

Bonnie realized she was whining, so before Mel could utter a single word, Bonnie began talking faster than a runaway freight train. She kept right on drilling Mel with questions. "Hidden treasure? What hidden treasure? Mel, you better start talking. Do you think I am going to save your life from some nasty old well full of mud and mosquitoes without you making me your equal partner and splitting the treasure with me? I won't let you, Mr. Mel."

Mel carefully placed his hand over little Bonnie's mouth, and he said, "Could you shut up long enough for me to tell you what I know? But first, you must swear, Bonnie, that anything I tell you, you will keep a secret. You must promise to do so, and lighting will strike you dead if you break your promise."

Bonnie was pretty smart. She said, "Only if you promise to share any treasure that we find. Do you?"

"I promise."

"I promise, too."

Mel and Bonnie shook hands. Bonnie began to talk. Again, Mel quickly put his hand over little Bonnie's mouth.

"Let me tell you about my grandpa, Bonnie. Then you will understand why I was down in the well. After the first attempt, I know it will be good to have your help. So just listen, and I will tell you all I know. It will be our secret, because my grandpa is dead, and it will be up to you and me to find the map that will lead us to the hidden treasure, which soon will be mine—I mean, ours," Mel quickly corrected himself."

Little Bonnie motioned Mel to continue. She was not going to mumble a sound until she had heard Mel P. Dread, her new friend, tell his story, although keeping her mouth closed was very hard for her to do!

Mel began to explain how he had gone on to live with his grandfather on his farm, where the old well was. After a few years, his grandfather became very ill. Mel did everything he could for him, and near the end, during the last week or so of his life, he was so delirious that Mel could not understand much of what his grandfather was mumbling.

"What did he say?" Bonnie started to ask.

Mel chimed in. "I will tell you what he said. He said 'Nap, nap!' He said 'nap' all the time."

Bonnie couldn't help but say, "The poor old guy was tired.

Maybe your grandpa just wanted to sleep."

"But it was just a few days ago that I realized it was not 'nap' Grandpa was saying. It was 'map.' He also kept saying 'well,' and I would say, 'No, Grandpa, you're not well. Now try to take a nap!' Bonnie, I think he was trying to tell me that the map was in the well." "What makes you think, Mel Dread, if you allow me to inquire, that he was talking about a treasure map and not a map of this here great United States of America?" she politely asked.

Mel said,"Grandpa would often speak of how his great-grand-father had, at a very young age, somehow discovered a ton of gold. Being a good Christian man, he hid the gold—or it disappeared No one knows for sure. The gold was never seen again. My Grandpa often said that someday someone would find the treasure and be wealthy beyond all belief.

Bonnie opened her mouth and said, "Now what do we do, Mel P. Dread?"

"We get some sleep. First thing in the morning, we will go back to the well and take another look."

Bonnie's grandmother was standing at the front door. She said, "Bonnie, come inside before you get eaten alive by mosquitoes, and tell that boy you're speaking to that it's been a long day. It's time for young people like him to be in bed."

Mel could not agree more as he said good night to Bonnie. He reminded her not to breathe a word of the story to anyone. They agreed to meet the next day at sunup.

"Tomorrow's Sunday, and I cannot miss church, so we will have to work fast to get back out to the well and find what we are looking for in time get home, clean up, and make it to church." They both agreed it was a plan, although Bonnie had not a clue about what they would be looking for.

CHAPTER 2

Pigs in a Blanket or Well, What Did You Find?

M el's new friend, Bonnie, was willing to assist Mel, and she would be an excellent investigative assistant. But one thing was for certain: She had no intention of going into that well. She would hold her position up top, where there was less mud, fewer bugs, and a lot less to worry about. *Treasure hunting is fun,* she thought. *What should I wear?*

It was still dark out when Mel crawled out of bed. Quietly he got dressed and grabbed his backpack. He hoped his partner, Bonnie, would be up and getting ready to go out to the old well and look for buried treasure. Just then there was a knock on his window. It was, of course, little Bonnie tossing pebbles at his window. She was bright-eyed and awake. She had hardly slept a wink. Finding the treasure was all she could think about. She wore her work boots, Levi's jeans with the cuffs rolled up, and her favorite sweatshirt, which said "I Have a Dream" and had Martin Luther King Jr.'s picture stenciled in black and white on it. She, too, had a dream, and she was ready to look for it.

Mel slipped out the back door, grabbing a big handful of cookies. He knew a little breakfast would help the two of them muster up the courage to go back down the well, where surely his grandpa had been telling him to look for something—something he had not noticed the first time he was down in that cold, dark, muddy hole in the ground. Mel jumped on his bike, crammed his pocket full of cookies, and sped down the street. Little Bonnie was right behind him, pedaling as fast as she could with a cookie in her mouth. She worked hard to keep up to Mel, who was by now way ahead of her.

In about ten minutes, they were standing by the well, both munching on cookies and looking at one another. Bonnie, with a mouthful of cookies, handed Mel a flashlight. She tried to say, "Well, what are you waiting for?" but with a mouthful of cookies, it sounded more like, "Fachewuhatingfur?"

He knew exactly what she wanted to say: time was a-wasting. It was a Sunday morning, and they both knew they would have to hurry. Mel climbed up on the rock ledge, tied the rope around his waist, and slowly began his descent into the deep well once again. He could see the mud at the bottom of the well glistening from the reflection of his flashlight. Soon he reached the bottom of the well. Bonnie up top yelled, "What do you see, Mel? Talk to me."

Bonnie could not contain her excitement.

Mel yelled back, "I see nothing, just rock walls, and I am standing knee deep in mud!"

"Are you sure?" Bonnie asked, yelling down the well shaft.

Just then Mel noticed a rock in the well wall with a big X scratched deep in its surface. He had found something, but what? Using his jackknife, he began digging the mortar out. Slowly, he began to pull the rock out of the well wall.

Bonnie was still up top, yelling, "Talk to me, Mel P. Dread. Talk to me!"

He replied, "I found something!"

Pointing the flashlight into the hole where the rock used to be, he could only see what looked like a pig. He reached in slowly. Sure enough, he pulled out a dusty old piggy bank. Shining the flashlight up the well shaft, Mel yelled, "It's a piggy bank!"

A piggy bank? Puzzled Bonnie thought for a moment and then yelled back, "I hope it's a big piggy bank, Mel P. Dread."

He wrapped the bank in his long-sleeved shirt, tucked it inside his T-shirt, and began the long climb up the rope where Bonnie was waiting with less optimism about being rich. After all, how much money could a piggy bank hold? Five, maybe six dollars in pennies or twelve, maybe, if it were nickels? Then she realized there could be silver dollars in the bank, and in that case she calculated it could hold maybe twenty-five dollars, max.

"Don't just stand there, Bonnie. There's a reason I refer to you as my assistant."

"Sorry," Bonnie said as she took Mel's arm and helped pull him out of the well.

Mel pulled the piggy bank out from under his T-shirt and laid it on the ground. Slowly he unwrapped it, wondering how long it had been since the piggy bank had last seen daylight. Thinking of daylight, Mel looked at his watch. Church would soon be starting, and they had no more time to ponder what they had just found, what it meant, and what secrets it may contain.

Mel and Bonnie, as fast as any superhero, made it home and managed to get cleaned up and dressed in just enough time to slip into the last row, far in the back, before the big church doors were pulled shut.

It seemed to be taking hours. First came the welcome and then more singing—blab, blab, blab. Then Mel's father, the minister, stood up and greeted everyone. He said, "Especially my son, who knows where he should be every Sabbath, where we should all be: giving praise to God who loves each and every one of us, the rich as well as the poor."

Mel and little Bonnie were sitting in the very last set of pews, paying little attention as Mel's father greeted his congregation by saying, "It is good to see each and every one of you this fine Sunday morning. Today I want you all to trust that God loves each of us, rich or poor; he loves the healthy and the sick."

Bonnie whispered to Mel, What do you think is in the piggy bank?" Mel and little Bonnie did not hear a word about the rich, the poor, the sick, the healthy, love, or salvation. All they heard was the word "amen" and the big wooden church doors being opened behind them. They wanted to be first out the door before anyone, especially Mel's father, could start asking all kinds of questions. Besides, both Mel and little Bonnie had sworn they would tell no one about the treasure, and that's how they planned to keep it.

Soon they were back in Mel's bedroom, where Mel carefully unwrapped the mysterious piggy bank. Bonnie impatiently bit her lip and waited.

It was a piggy bank for sure, Mel deduced, as there was a coin slot on the top of the pig's back. "Bonnie," he said, "would you please hand me my big magnifying glass?"

The magnifying glass lay next to the big jar of marbles Mel had been collecting all his life. She quickly did what Mel asked. Mel held the magnifying glass over what appeared to be something printed on the side of the piggy bank.

"Well," Bonnie chimed in, "what does it say?"

"Iowa Territorial Bank, 149 Main Street, claim number 457, Des Moines County." Mel read it again.

Bonnie grabbed the piggy bank and started shaking it. She could tell that there was something in the bank. She tipped it upside down and shook it even harder. Mel, in shock, just stared at little Bonnie.

"Mel," she shouted. "Can't you hear that there is something inside this pig?" Just then the bank popped out of little Bonnie's hands. The bank was now in the air, in free fall. In total disbelief, they could only watch as the piggy bank hit the hard wooden floor of Mel's bedroom. The piggy bank lay on the floor, shattered into several pieces.

"Oh my," Bonnie said, covering her mouth with both hands in horror. "Money!" There among the broken pieces of what was once a piggy bank lay three coins and a little silver key. They each picked one up.

Mel said, "Not just coins, Bonnie. Gold coins!

Bonnie said, "Not only gold coins, Mel. There is a key as well." Mel looked at the key Bonnie held in her hand. Mel knew something about these gold coins. They were old, and with some ood detective work Mel P. Dread would solve this mystery.

He smiled at little Bonnie and said, "Thanks for all your help. You are the best assistant a good private investigator could ever hope to have."

Bonnie smiled back, laughing, and she said, "I do my best."

Mel was laughing too. He thought finding a small treasure was more fun than he ever could have imagined. The best treasure he had was little Bonnie as his assistant. More importantly, they were becoming friends. Mel knew that rich or poor, happy or sad, the two of them were a perfect team.

"Let's clean this mess up," Bonnie said, "get something to eat, and figure out where we go next."

They were both thinking where it might be. Mel was already thinking about a trip to their neighboring state to investigate the Iowa Territorial

Bank at 149 Main Street in Des Moines County. He had so many questions, but they would have to wait.

They were both hungry, and it had been a very exciting Sunday for sure. Hiding the coins in his big jar of marbles, they both ran down the stairs. Mel knew that he could find at least a couple of colas and a bag of potato chips. They headed for the front porch to open the bag of chips and lick the salt off their moist fingers.

With a mouthful of chips, little Bonnie asked Mel, "Do you really think God loves all of us the same?"

Mel just smiled and said, "Maybe!"

Mel tried to sleep, but he could not. All he could think about were those three gold coins. He got out his flashlight from under his bed, where he always kept a spare in case the lights went out or he wanted to investigate in the dark of night, like now. Mel carefully unburied the three gold coins he had hidden in his collection of marbles. He knew these coins were very old, and he handled them with the utmost respect. He could see they had been minted, as they were all perfectly the same: same color, same weight, and the same markings on each side.

He laid one of the three gold coins on the bed face up. He laid the second coin on the bed next to it with the back side up. The flashlight made the coins shine as if they were alive, and the reflection seemed to dazzle Mel's eyes. He quickly put his hand over the flashlight's end. Everything went dark, except the pink glow of Mel's hand covering the light.

He laid the flashlight down, picked up a coin, and held it where it could not shine so intensely. With his trusty magnifying glass, he could see the face of a man on the front. It had stars around the outside edge—thirteen, to be exact—and at the bottom between the rows of stars was the year 1855. He turned the coin over. He saw the United States of America's eagle crest, and around the outside edge he could read "United States of America." Mel knew that the coins were valuable, and first thing tomorrow he would go down to the country road mall. Mel knew the owner of Clyde's Gold for Cash Shop, where they advertised that they bought antique coins. It said that right on the front window, he thought, as he held the coins in the palm of his hand. He turned off the flashlight and fell asleep, still clinging to the three gold coins. He thought of Bonnie and wondered if she was asleep.

Bonnie was across the street falling asleep as well, wondering, too, if her new best friend, Mel, was in his bed and was asleep as well. "Good night, Mel," little Bonnie said as she took one last look at the clock. It was exactly midnight. Back across the street, Mel too looked at his alarm clock.

"Good night, Bonnie." He pulled the sheet up to his chin, smiled, and added, "I will see you in my dreams."

Soon they both were fast asleep, and as one would expect, they both had dreams. Mel called dreams visions, messages from dead people such as his grandparents. That night Mel saw his grandfather. It did not seem like a dream, and yet it must be, as he was standing in an old cemetery, in front of a headstone. Mel could see the carved tombstone. How could he not wake up and remember exactly what it read? It said, "Here lay Mel P. Dread, 1822–1902, Husband, and Bonnie Lou Dread, 1822–1902, Wife." Chiseled in smaller print was, "God loves both the poor as well as the rich."

The sun was shining in Mel's bedroom window, and he could hear little Bonnie outside yelling as softly as she could. "Mel, Mel P. Dread, you still in bed? Mel! Mel!" she yelled a little more loudly.

Pulling back the curtain, Mel hollered back "Just woke up! Yeah, ok, just give me a few minutes to get dressed." They simultaneously gave each other the thumb -up.

Grabbing his pants and running down the hall to brush his teeth and do his morning business, Mel slapped on some of his dad's aftershave, put on his baseball cap, and thought once again that with his good luck he would miss his father, who was usually in his study reading his Bible and having his morning tea at this time.

"I am surprised," Mel said to little Bonnie, "my father did not hear you this early in the morning. We need to get a better way to communicate."

"Right on," Bonnie replied. "Our very own cell phones. When we find the treasure, I will be the richest twelve-year-old girl in the world. I think I will be able to afford to get us cell phones—bright pink cell phones."

Mel looked at her and asked, "Pink? Why would anyone want a pink cell phone?"

Bonnie laughed. "You're right, Mel. We said we would split everything fifty-fifty, so instead of pink cell phones, let's compromise. Pink is for girls and blue is for boys, so our new cell phones will be purple."

She looked around and could see Mel riding down the street toward the Country Town Mall. He was off to see Darrell of Clyde's Gold for Cash store. Jumping on her bike, she soon caught up to Mel. The first thing out of Bonnie's mouth was, "Purple, Mel. I don't think you were listening."

"Purple gives me goose bumps," he yelled over his shoulder He then said, as nicely as he could, "Bonnie, could you punch back into work and do what assistants are supposed to do? Jus stand there within my sight quietly and wait until I ask you for your assistance. Do you comprehend what I, Mr. Mel P. Dread, private investigator, requires of you at this very moment?"

Little Bonnie nodded her head and mimed her rendition of the old zipping-up-one's-lips act. With one big gesture, she threw the imaginary key over her shoulder.

"Good!" Mel opened the shop door. He could see Darrell drinking coffee at the back of the store, where he also lived. "Hello, Darrell. It's your friend Mel Dread. A long time no see," he said as he reached out to shake Darrell's hand.

"It certainly has been a while, Mel. What brings you to see me?" Darrell asked. "Looking at gold rings?"

Bonnie smiled politely. "No," Mel said. "My grandfather left me a gold coin, and I thought maybe you could tell me what it was worth." "What year is it?" Darrell asked as he sipped on his coffee while petting his old dog, which was mostly blind and lying in his lap. "1855," Mel said.

"I suppose you might let me take a look at this gold coin, wouldn't you?" Darrell said as he took another sip of his coffee.

Mel reached into his backpack where he had safely placed the coin in a zippered pocket. "Sure," Mel said, handing him the coin. Darrell, without much hesitation, said "Minted gold, 1855. Very rare coin you got here, Mel."

"How much do you think I could get for it?" Mel asked timidly, knowing Darrell would offer him much less than what the coin was really worth. Darrell quickly transferred the information off the coin into his computer, and immediately there on the screen appeared a photo of the same coin.

Darrell began to read out loud, "This rare gold coin minted in 1855 is one of many thousands that were lost and never found. It is estimated there are only five or six of these gold coins in existence. The United States Mint was shipping the approximately one ton of gold coins by horse-drawn wagons to the newly built Iowa Territorial Bank in the city of Des Moines, Iowa. When the gold arrived in Iowa, the armed guards swore the ton of gold coins had never left their sight.

"It was moved by United States officials from the wagon directly into the bank vault. There it was under lock and key, with armed guards standing outside the vault. The next day when they opened the vault and pried open the crates, all they found were four crates full of bags of rocks. A ton of gold coins was nowhere to be found."

Darrell looked deep into Mel's baby blue eyes, paused, and then said, "You know, Mel, I consider you a friend. That said, I am prepared to offer you five hundred dollars for it." Mel picked up the gold coin and put it securely in his backp ck. Throwing the backpack over his left shoulder, Mel said in a professional voice, "I think I will hang on to it for the time being, my friend."

Bonnie looke over her shoulder at Darrell and repeated, "Yes, we think we will han on to it for the time being." She followed Mel out the front door.

They were barely out the door of Clyde's Gold for Cash Shop when Mel heard little Bonnie's mouth open as she took a big gasp of air and let it out in a gale-force wind. "Whiss!"

Mel knew the sound.

"Oh! That is a small fortune," little Bonnie yelled. "Five hundred bucks? Mel, what the heck are you thinking—or were you thinking, Mel? You did not even ask me for my opinion. Not once did you consult with me. Mel P. Dread, you said everything would be spilt fifty-fifty. Mel, are you listening to me?" She gasped. She had run out of air, and her face had turned a bit blue in color.

"I heard every word," Mel replied. "You're absolutely right." Mounting his bicycle, Mel yelled, "Race you to the library!"

Once again Bonnie was left in Mel P. Dread's dust. Mounting her bike, she was doing the math: half of three gold coins would only equal $750. Mel was right. No deal!

When Mel arrived at the library, Bonnie was still a few blocks away. Mel did not wait. When Bonnie finally found Mel, he was in the library basement looking at old maps of Nebraska and Iowa. Mel was looking for anything to do with the Iowa Territorial Bank of Des Moines.

Bonnie plopped down in a large wooden library chair and said, "If you need me, I will be right here." She laid her head on the big wooden table and was soon fast asleep.

Mel thought to himself, *Good, let her sleep!* Pulling his notepad and pencil out of his backpack, he began to read and make extensive, detailed notes.

It had been a good couple of hours when Bonnie finally tipped her head up, gazed over at Mel with one eye, and said, "Have they brought us our food yet?" Raising her head and sniffing the air, little Bonnie exclaimed, "This restaurant smells like it's in the basement of a stinky old library."

Sitting up straight in the big wooden chair, she was trying to wake herself up by rubbing her eyes with her fists. Giggling, Bonnie said to Mel, "Now where did I leave off?" Little Bonnie was still trying to get Mel to laugh while Mel gathered up his notebook, filled with sketches and drawings and stuff that only a professional private investigator could possibly make any sense of, and then turned and walked away. Bonnie, trying to give her last, best shot at being funny, stood at the bottom of the stairs and asked Mel, "Do you think these steps go up?" Mel looked at her and replied, "Now, don't you fret about difficult matters like whether or not these stairs go up or down. I would never expect any newly acquired assistant to know which direction she was going, let alone understand the principles of steps!"

Chuckling to himself, Mel looked at little Bonnie, still standing at the bottom of the basement stairs, and continued, "I will make all the hard calculations. For now let's go home and fix some lunch." "Your house or mine?" Bonnie asked. Mel, not taking the middle-of-the-road position, answered her with, "Let's see what your grandma's got to eat."

"Sounds like a plan! I am right behind you." In almost every situation, Bonnie was.

Their lunch was good old peanut butter and homemade strawberry jam sandwiches, ice cold lemonade, and Salty Dog potato chips with dill pickles. They each ate two peanut butter and jelly sandwiches. As Mel was working on getting dill pickles and potato chips between the two pieces of white bread spread with peanut butter and strawberry jam, Bonnie asked, "Do you have a name for that sandwich?"

Mel thought. "I proclaim this the End World Hunger sandwich," he said as he proceeded to take a big bite out of his latest creation. Right now, hunger was on his mind.

"I think I have a plan," Mel said.

Bonnie looked at him and said, "Mel, how are we going to get to Iowa?"

"By bus," Mel replied. Chugging his cold lemonade, he said, "You don't have to come if you are too afraid."

"Afraid!" Bonnie blurted out, choking on her sandwich. "Mel P. Dread, I may be a girl, and your bike may be newer and faster than mine, but a deal's a deal."

"A deal is a deal?" Mel asked, a bit confused about what that had to do about being afraid. Besides, Mel had only said that to see how little Bonnie would react.

"Yes," Bonnie said, lowering her voice. "We agreed on splitting the treasure fifty-fifty, and that means my getting beyond any comprehensions that I may have."

Mel interrupted Bonnie. "I think you mean apprehensions, not comprehensions."

Bonnie looked at Mel and said "Whatever!"

Mel smiled at her. He was a little afraid as well, but as a professional private eye, he tried very hard to never let his fear get the best of him. He also knew that having Bonnie by his side would make the trip to Des Moines more fun.

"Finish eating," Mel said as he pulled another dill pickle out of the jar and, quicker than a lightning strike, stuck it in Bonnie's mouth. Then he added, "That's a good look for you. Now eat your dill pickle and let's go."

* * *

Little Bonnie's mother and father were spending the weekend with Bonnie and her grandmother. It was the middle of the summer, and, as during the past couple of summers, her parents had driven for six and a half hours to visit for the weekend. Bonnie's parents would return again in about four more weeks to take Bonnie back home to, Springerville, known for its chicken processing plants. Yes, it was known for chicken processing plants—of all things for a town to be known for, little Bonnie thought.

Little Bonnie had grown up around poultry farmers, and chickens were the pride of her hometown. "There's more to the chicken then meets the eye," her father would say to Bonnie.

Bonnie could remember her father telling her, "It starts with the egg." Then came fresh eggs, pickled eggs, liquid eggs, dehydrated eggs. The egg was big business—a business designed and devoted to the exploitation of the egg, Bonnie often thought. Then there were, of course, the eggs that were used to hatch baby chickens, millions of them. Millions upon millions of cute, fuzzy little chickens grew into young, tender-breasted, juicy birds. When they reach their optimal weight, those birds are processed into lunch meat, hot dogs, chicken pieces, whole fryers, or ground meat. The birds are frozen, canned, and dried, and anything that is left over gets used. Used in making dog food and cat food, chicken meat is dried, canned, and shipped around the world. The feathers are used to stuff pillows and quilts and sold to craft stores. Bonnie's mind was going a mile a minute, and knew she had better sit down. She sat patiently waiting on her grandmother's overstuffed couch, which faced the picture window overlooking the driveway. She expected to see her parents' van show up soon. Her grandma was in the kitchen fixing lunch. Grandma knew that her son, little Bonnie's dad, loved his mom's chicken pot pies. She could hear her grandmother move into the dining room, busily setting the table. Bonnie could see Mel's father sitting on his front porch, but there was no sign of Mel. Bonnie knew Mel had lots to plan if he was going to figure out how the two of them were to get to Iowa. She tried to remember where they were going in Iowa, but at the moment she had also forgotten what was to be found there. Plus, she wondered, without selling one of those gold coins, where did Mel expect to come up with enough cash to get them to Iowa?

The sound of a car horn blowing startled Bonnie. It was her dad pulling into the driveway, and as always he had a big grin on his face. Grandma had been standing by the front door waiting, and little Bonnie had not noticed her there. She ran down the steps and gave her dad and her mother a big hug. She could see Mel across the street talking to his father. She wondered if Mel already knew what he was planning. As always, she would have to wait and wonder. Bonnie took her dad's hand, saying, "Guess what, Dad? Grandma made your favorite food. Can you guess what it is?"

"Well, if I know my mom as well as I think I do, I'll bet it's her famous chicken pot pie."

Grandma interrupted by saying, "Wash your hands and come sit down. Chicken pot pie is best at room temperature."

Bonnie interrupted, "The last dishes!" one to the table has to do the Mel waved at his friend across the street. Bonnie did not see him as she was busy rushing up the stairs, out of his sight. Mel listened to his father as he said, "It sure is good to see you have found a friend, even if is only for a few more weeks. Then it's back to school for the both of you. This year, Mel, I know you will be an A student and make me proud to be your father."

Mel thought, *If I can just find my grandpa's lost treasure, I know then my dad will be proud of me, regardless of my grades!*

"Gone? Back up," Mel said to his father. "Did you just tell me you will be gone?"

"Yes," his father replied. "I am going to a Christian gathering of state pastors for most of this next week. You have to pay more attention. That's why your teachers do not like you. You never pay attention. You're always somewhere in your head, daydreaming."

Mel was trying to listen to what his father was saying but was not doing a very good job. What did his father mean that his teachers did not like him? The part about not paying attention was one hundred percent right, though, Mel thought.

"How long will you be gone?" Mel asked?

"I just told you, Mel. I leave tomorrow morning, Monday, and I will be back next Friday. And on the following Sunday, I do expect to see you in church. Did you hear me, Mel?" his father sternly asked.

"Yes, I know. Don't get into trouble, because it won't reflect well on you and all those lost souls who come to hear you preach every Sunday morning!" Mel said, smiling.

His father smiled back. "You have my cell phone number.

Don't hesitate to call if you need to.

Mel chirped in, "Listen, Dad, not to worry. Bonnie and I will hang out during the day, and at night I will watch some TV and eat good, healthy junk food to keep myself from starvation."

"Here, Mel," his father said, taking out his wallet and handing Mel three ten-dollar bills. He also handed Mel one of his extra credit cards. With the voice of an overindulging preacher, he started to lecture Mel some more, saying, "Do not use my credit card except for special emergencies. Also, son, please try not to spend all the cash I have given you. You need to learn how to handle money better then you currently do, Mel P. Dread."

Mel answered, "Thanks, Dad. I heard every word you said." Then Mel ran as fast as he could up the stairs to his bedroom, quickly closing the door behind him Mel pumped his fist and high fived himself. *How perfect,* he thought. He would travel to Des Moines, Iowa, alone if he could not somehow convince or drag his new best friend, Bonnie, along with him. Mel laughed to himself at the thought of trying to drag little Bonnie anywhere. Mel had two days to design and craft the plans. He knew that tomorrow when he saw Bonnie during church service, she would be desperate to be informed about his newest plans.

He began laying out maps of Nebraska and Iowa. It was a hobby of Mel's to collect books, maps, and, of course, his monthly copies of *Private Eye* magazine. He had collected every copy, even those from before he was born. Pinning the Nebraska map onto his bedroom wall, he took a red push pin and stuck it into the map where he was: Ainsworth, Nebraska. He then placed the Iowa map next to the Nebraska map and lined up Interstate Highway 80.

Pushing in more pins to hold the map on the wall, Mel searched the Iowa map for the city of Des Moines. He followed Highway 80 east. Big as life, not far past Iowa City, there was the city he would soon visit. "Des Moines," he said as he plunged a yellow push pin into the map covering the "Des," leaving only the "Moines" showing. Mel quickly removed the yellow pin and replunged it, this time where he wanted it to be.

He would leave the maps pinned to his bedroom wall. If something awful should happen to him and Bonnie, he wanted to leave a trail for his dad and the police to follow. He dug into his backpack and found what he had copied down from the piggy bank's side before Bonnie dropped it on the floor. With the note in his hand he read out loud, "Iowa Territorial Bank, 149 Main Street, Des Moines, Iowa, claim number 457, grand opening 1899."

It was dark out, and across the street little Bonnie was saying her prayers. Bonnie ended her prayers with, "Please keep us both safe, dear God." Then she added, "I think we may need all the help we can get! Amen!"

You could hear the organ playing and the bells ringing in the church steeple. Most people were already in the church and sitting down. Mel waited as Bonnie and her family walked up the sidewalk. Bonnie spotted Mel, too, and announced to her family that she was going to sit with him.

Grandma said, "Sure, sweetie. Nothing wrong with having a crush on the preacher's son. And that Mel is quite the looker, too," she added.

Bonnie slid in next to Mel. They did not say a word, just turned the hymnal to page 143 and began to sing, "Bringing in the sheaves, bringing in the sheaves, we will come rejoicing, bringing in the sheaves." Mel, without losing a beat, handed Bonnie a note from inside his coat pocket.

Bonnie was distracted by the note. She began singing, "Bringing in the sheep." Mel poked her with his elbow and pointed to the word sheaves, giggling. Then he started singing, "Bringing in the sheep."

As he was singing, Mel was thinking about how it would be when Bonnie was gone, when summer would be over and he would once again be mostly alone and lonely. Mel had drifted into a mental silent void. He was suddenly awoken by his father's words.

Mel's father was preaching about how it takes a village to raise a child and we each must do our part to give, not only with our hearts but with our wallets as well. Mel took out two dollar bills, handed one to Bonnie, and waited for the donation plate to come by them. Mel looked at Bonnie and, giggling, whispered, "It is okay; there is a lot more money where this came from."

Little Bonnie reluctantly gave up the dollar and placed it on top of all the other money in the offering plate.

Mel leaned over to little Bonnie and he whispered, "Have a nice day. Read my note and meet me tonight on my front porch about six o'clock." Mel winked at her and smiled.

"Praise God from whom all blessings come, Praise each and every one, Praise be to all mankind..." Mel handed the hymnal to little Bonnie and, without making as much as a sound, was out the side door of the church. Jumping on his bike, he headed for home. Mel felt confident he not only could but would get to Des Moines, Iowa, but then what? Grabbing a bag of chips and a cold beverage from the refrigerator, Mel headed to his bedroom. There he would spend the afternoon trying to put together the pieces of the puzzling mystery involving gold coins from the year 1855, a mysterious key, and a treasure map he had not yet found—or, as his grandfather called it, the treasure nap.

Mel missed his grandfather and thought of him constantly. It was almost as if his grandfather were there with Mel nearly all the time, and that was a very good feeling. Mel wanted to make his grandfather happy by finding the treasure map that would lead to more old gold coins, the treasure his grandfather had been so desperately trying to tell him about in the last few days of his life.

Tearing open the chip bag, Mel snapped open the cold drink, lifted the can in the air, and made a symbolic toast, saying, "Here's to the poor, here's to the rich. If you don't have much money, life can be a real…"

That is what Mel had long ago concluded. Picking up his cola, he turned on his computer and thought, *Where should I begin?* Thinking, he said out loud, "How would one get to Des Moines, Iowa?"

He found that three daily buses ran along Highway 80. All they would need to do, assuming Bonnie would able to be his travel partner, would be find a ride down to Highway 80 and catch a bus. The bus would take them straight across Nebraska and though Iowa to Des Moines. It would take the two of them about seven hours to reach their destination. They would return the same way. Mel thought, *This is going to be a piece of cake.* Everything was falling into place. He started singing, "Thank God from whom all blessings come," hoping that somehow he and little Bonnie would be blessed with gold coins, lots and lots of gold coins.

Mel heard his father yell up the stairway, "Mel, you have a good week. You be a good boy, and for Pete's sake, be sure not to do anything foolish. Stay close to home."

Mel yelled back, "I will be fine. Not to worry, Dad. You know I try to always remember that you are the pastor of a renowned local Christian church and how I behave reflects upon your position in the community."

Before Mel was finished, his father replied, "See you in a week, Son."

Mel heard the door shut and saw his father's station wagon pulling out of the driveway. It was an older car with green, faded paint, still in good shape, with one bumper sticker that read, "Jesus loves the poor as well as the rich" and another one that read, "My son is an honor student at Ainsworth Junior High."

His father was far, far down the road when Mel could hear little Bonnie out dragging a stick across the front picket fence, making a clicking sound. He opened his window and motioned Bonnie to come upstairs. Dropping the stick, Bonnie ran up the stairs, closing the door behind her and locking the latch.

Mel stood at the top of the stairs and asked politely, "Bonnie, would you get a couple of bottles of water out of the ice box? Oh, and would you also please bring that box of chocolate shortbread cookies on the kitchen counter? Thanks!"

Bonnie added, "Yes, it's important to eat a well-balanced, nutritious meal." She laughed as she ran up the stairs. After handing the cookies and a bottle of water to Mel, little Bonnie leaped into the air and landed on Mel's soft bed, landing with a soft poof on her back. She snuggled down into Mel's down-filled tick, which was once his great-grandfather's.

"Well," she said, "I read your note, and I did exactly what you told me to do. I looked her right in the eyes and told her I would like to attend Bible camp this week. I lied to her, just like your note said to do. I let her believe there would be lots of adult chaperones, including your dad, and that you would also be there."

"What did she say, Bonnie?" Mel asked slowly, not knowing what to expect.

"She said... well, she said," Bonnie said with a sad expression, "She said yes!" Mel took a deep breath and said, "Wow!"

"Okay," Mel said to little Bonnie. "You be here tomorrow morning. Bring everything you would need for a week at Bible school. We do not want your grandmother to be suspicious of a thing. Bring your backpack, too, but only pack your back ack with what you will be taking with us to Des Moines, as we will leave your suitcases here in my bedroom. I plan to pack one backpack as well." Mel assured Bonnie that that would be all they would need. "Tomorrow morning we are going to do whatever it takes to get to Des Moines," Mel said. He and little Bonnie high fived each other, both ready for the new adventure that awaited them in the morning.

Daydreaming Bonnie softly said, "Des Moines." Then she repeated in an annoyingly bad French accent, "Des Moines."

Turning to Mel, still in the same annoyingly bad French accent, she asked, "Dear Inspector Dread, just how are we going to get to Des Moines, Iowa?"

Mel replied, "Walk, hitchhike, take a bus, ride in a taxi, maybe take a ride in the park in one of those horse-drawn carriages. We will eat in the finest restaurants; we'll drink fine imported bottled water, and maybe we'll spend the day at the local spa for a mud bath."

"Mud bath!" Bonnie squealed. "Now I know you're pulling my leg, Mel! Tell me the truth, Mr. Mel P. Dread!"

Mel looked at little Bonnie and said, "For now, all you need to do is go home, get packed, and be back here at seven a.m." Bonnie picked up her bottle of water and a handful of cookies and headed home without a word.

Bonnie knew Mel well enough to know that he would tell her, but not until he had come up with a better plan. Little Bonnie was not at all convinced that Mel had any plan yet to locate any lost treasure. She was still concerned about how Mel would get them to Des Moines, Iowa.

"See you the morning," Mel said as he followed little Bonnie down the stairs and, like a true gentleman, opened the front door for her.

Bonnie leaned over and blew a kiss toward Mel. "Try to get some sleep. I know that as long as we are friends, things will be okay! It does not matter what we find or do not find. Mr. Melvin P. Dread, I know before anything else, it is our friendship that is and will remain priceless."

It was a long night for Mel, who spent much of it taking notes and gathering any information off the Internet that he thought might be useful. He made as many mental notes as he could in such a short amount of time. He was actually learning a great deal. The question was, how much of it would be of help in finding the treasure?

Mel finished packing. It was almost 6:00 a.m., and he could hear the neighbor's rooster crowing. The sun was just breaking through the trees and lighting up his room. He could hear a knock on the front door. *Well,* he thought, *little Bonnie is right on time.* Dragging his overpacked backpack down the stairs, he unlocked the door to let Bonnie in. She was standing there with two big suitcases and her overstuffed backpack.

Mel said, "Come in, milady. Allow me to get your bags." Bonnie, managing her backpack, stepped inside, saying,

"Thank you, Mel P. Dread… so very kind of you."

Mel grabbed the handles of the two big suitcases and with all his might lifted them up. Mel began laughing and said, "These suitcases are too light to have anything in them."

She looked right back at Mel and said to him, "Did you really think I was going to fill up two big suitcases and haul them over here to your house, only to leave them here for a week and then haul them back across the street again? Do you, Mel P. Dread, think I am that empty headed? Well, do you?"

Mel headed up the stairs, carrying the empty suitcases, while Bonnie yelled to him, laughing,"Just throw them anywhere. What's for breakfast, Mel?"

Mel grabbed a couple of juice boxes from the refrigerator and a box of prewrapped individual Rice Krispie Treats from the pantry.

Mel tossed a Rice Krispie Treat across the kitchen, hitting Little Bonnie in the head. Looking down to see what Mel had thrown at her, she gasped. "Oh my Gawd, Rice Krispie Treats. Priceless!" she said.

Mel motioned for her to pick up her backpack and opened the front door, saying, "We need to get over to the highway."

Bonnie looked at him and said, "You're not planning to hitch-hike all the way to Des Moines, Iowa?"

"No," Mel said. "Just down to Interstate 80, where we will catch the Route 80 bus, which will take us all the way to Des Moines."

It was not long before they were standing at the edge of town. As it was still early, there was not a lot of traffic. Mel and Bonnie wasted the time eating Rice Krispie Treats and pra ticing how to stick out their thumbs each time a car would go by. Finally, what looked to be an old farm truck pulled over to give them a ride. Happily, they ran to get into the truck.

Mel opened the truck door, and Bonnie climbed into the truck's cab. Mel nudged her to scoot her butt over on the old, weathered leather seat. She said, "Hello, my name's Bonnie, and this is my brother, Mel." She continued with, "We are so thankful that you stopped to give us a ride. We are headed to catch a bus to Des Moines, Iowa, where my brother, Mel, and I will visit our grandmother. Our grandmother is alone and in very bad health, and she is in need of our help."

Mel just listened to Bonnie as they drove south to Highway 80. Mel began to wonder if the old man was hard of hearing, so in a loud voice he asked the man what his name was. The old man did not turn his head. He just kept his eyes on the road until he reached the junction with Highway 80, where he pulled over and let them out. They both got out of the truck and waved good-bye as the old man turned west and drove off.

CHAPTER 3

One Way or Round Trip? or Iowa Be Home in about a Week

They could see a sign that read, "Bus Route 80 stop #53 east to Iowa. Pick-up times Mon–Sun 9 a.m., 12 p.m., 6:30 p.m., except on holidays or during bad weather."

There was a bench to sit down on while waiting. About one hour after they arrived, a big purple and red bus pulled up and the bus's big metal door opened up. "Where are you headed?" the balding bus driver asked as he stroked his long, black beard.

Mel said, "My sister and I are traveling to the city of Des Moines."

The bus driver said, "Well, welcome aboard. Would you like round-trip tickets?"

"Round trip," Mel answered the bus driver.

"Today is your lucky day, mates," the driver replied. "Today it's 'Two Travel for the Price of One Day,' which means tickets for children twelve years or younger are half price. A round trip for the two of you is only fifteen dollars." Mel handed him twenty dollars. The bus driver handed Mel back two ticket stubs and a five-dollar bill.

"Hang on to those return tickets," he told them. The driver waited while they both struggled with their backpacks and found two empty seats near the back of the bus.

When he could see that they had both been seated, the driver yelled, "Next stop, Lincoln, Nebraska." The bus got back on Highway 80, heading east toward Iowa.

Looking around, Mel could see mostly older people. The bus smelled of disinfectant. He could see Bonnie looking around as well. He poked her and said, "What did you bring for us to eat?"

"Bring us to eat? Are you kidding me?" Bonnie asked, adding, "I could hardly get my clothes and other personal items in my small backpack, let alone find room to pack food." Looking at Mel with big eyes, little Bonnie announced, "Wait, I did too bring food." Unzipping a pocket in her backpack, she pulled out a bag of trail mix, a little box of mints, and a pack of gum.

"Ah ha," little Bonnie exclaimed. "Here I have some trail mix and assorted goodies. Let's see what you brought us to eat, Mr. Smarty Pants."

Mel unzipped his pack and pulled out a paper bag. Bonnie was already excited. She could not begin to guess what Mel would have brought them to eat. She knew she was feeling very hungry, and whatever Mel had in the paper sack would help take away her hunger pains. Mints, gum, and trail mix did not sound that appetizing to Bonnie.

Opening the bag, Mel took out two thick bologna sandwiches and gave one to Bonnie. Then he pulled out a plastic jar of dill pickles and said, "Bon appétit, ma cheri."

She replied, "Thank you. You have thought of everything, Mr. Mel P. Dread."

As the bus sped down Highway 80, they both ate their bologna sandwiches and munched on dill pickles. Somewhere in the middle of Bonnie telling Mel about her childhood, they both fell asleep. It was just what they both needed: some food and some rest. They would also need lots of luck when they pulled into the city of Des Moines in about five more hours. Mel heard the bus driver say "Lincoln, Nebraska," but went back to sleep.

A few hours later, the bus pulled into West Des Moines. "The next stop is where we get off," Mel said to Bonnie.

"How long?" Bonnie asked Just then the bus driver yelled, "Next stop, fifteen minutes. We will be in Des Moines, Iowa."

Having both used the bathroom in the back of the bus, they both agreed the experience was so far the worst they had had. They were both hoping and silently praying that their search for Grandpa's lost treasure would leave them both rich, unscathed, unharmed, and alive, with more money than either of them could even imagine. Then for their next trip they could take their private jet instead of someone else's bus.

Mel added, "Maybe when we find the treasure we should buy a spanking new RV."

"A private eye RV," Bonnie laughed. "Mel, have you forgotten that we both are still too young to drive?"

Mel responded, "Drive? I would have our people do the driving for us."

"Our people." They both laughed at that thought!

"Yes," Mel said to little Bonnie. "It's really how rich people live." Bonnie asked, "What about all the poor people?"

Mel shrugged his shoulders and said, "What about them?" "Downtown, Des Moines, six o'clock Eastern Standard Time. Enjoy your evening, folks. We appreciate that you all chose to travel with us. Please come back again soon," said the driver into his handheld microphone.

After they had helped each other drag their backpacks off the bus, Bonnie exclaimed, "Now what, Mr. Mel P. Dread, private eye mystery solving detective guy?"

Mel said, "We need to find a place to spend the night, order room service, and get an early start in the morning. That's all you need to think about right now, Miss Bonnie Lou Starr. Concentrate on maybe finding a room with double beds and a bathtub."

Walking over to a cab, Mel said to the driver, "I only have ten dollars and need to find a nice place to sleep for the night."

The cab driver opened the cab door. "Not a problem, kid," he replied. "Grab your girlfriend and hop in."

Mel handed the driver a ten-dollar bill. "What part of Des Moines you looking to go to?" asked the taxi driver.

Mel said, "Near 149 Main Street. Anywhere in that vicinity would be greatly appreciated, sir."

Bonnie did not say a word but just closed the door and squeezed Mel's hand tightly.

"Are you from around here?" the cab driver asked them. "We are here on business," Mel replied.

"Business? You don't look like the business type. Mind if I ask you what kind of business?" the cab driver asked Mel.

Mel answered slowly, with sadness in his voice. "Our mother left us when my sister and I were barely out of diapers." Mel had sat through enough of his father's Sunday sermons to know how to play the crowd. Putting his arm around little Bonnie, Mel said, "We'll find our mama. Everything will be alright, Sara Marie." He winked at Bonnie.

It did not seem they had gone all that far when the cab pulled up in front of a big church.

"Why are we stopping here?" asked Mel. The cab driver turned his body, throwing his arm over the cab seat. His arm was covered with tattoos. Mel replied, "Nice ink, man."

"Thanks, partner." The cab driver looked at them both sitting in the back of the cab. "Do you have a lot of money to spend on a motel room?" the cabby asked.

Bonnie answered first. "Honestly, sir, we are as poor as dirt." Mel repeated, "She's right. We're both poor as dirt!"

"This is the Christian homeless shelter. I stayed here many nights before I found this taxi cab job. There are clean bathrooms and clean showers. Everyone gets their own bed, but best of all is, they serve breakfast, a bag lunch, and a hot meal at night. I want to wish you the best of luck in finding your mother. One's mother is like lost treasure. Until you find it, you cannot ever truly find any rest. My name is on the card, so if you need a ride anywhere while you are visiting our fair city, the cab fare is on me. Like God," the cab driver added, "I love the rich as well as the poor." Handing back Mel's ten-dollar bill, he opened their door and let them out of the cab.

Mel and Bonnie both said, "We do not know how to thank you. You are a very kind man."

"The name's Mike, and I believe that I should always do unto others as I would have them do unto me. Now get inside! They close the doors at eight p.m. sharp." Mike's yellow cab slowly disappeared into the distance, out of sight.

They could see someone waiting at the top of the big stairs. It was a lady wearing a long dress, and it looked as though she was waiting to close the doors. Little Bonnie and Mel hurried up the steps and scooted inside. Behind them a voice said, "Welcome to our mission shelter," as she worked to close the big church doors behind them.

"My name is Mary Ann Leslie Claire. As you can see, we close the doors at eight sharp. Come this way and I will show you around briefly. The lights are turned off at eight forty-five sharp, without exception. The lights are turned on at five a.m., and we provide a warm breakfast from six until seven. Those requesting a bag lunch should ask for one at the beginning of breakfast and pick the bag lunch up before leaving for the day, making sure to take all of your personal belongs with you when you leave the shelter. We do have resource counselors available on request and will help with any minor medical concerns. Do you have any questions?" the lady asked.

"There's the men's bathroom," she said, pointing, "and the men's showers. There's the girls' bathroom and shower." She smiled down at little Bonnie. "We have cameras that keep surveillance twenty-four seven in most designated areas, and we have full-time staff. We keep a close eye on each one of our overnight guests." She led them over to two unoccupied cots and said, "Sleep well."

There were lots of cots, and only about half of them had people sleeping in them. Mel reasoned that it was because in the summer the homeless slept outside in the park.

They took turns using the bathroom, brushed their teeth, and thought about how g od a shower would feel in the morning.

Bonnie whispered to Mel as they lay down on their beds for the night, "Wow, did you ever think we would be spending the night in a homeless shelter in Des Moines, Iowa, looking for ga—oh."

"Shhh," Mel interrupted. "It's been a long day. Go to sleep!"

Bonnie whispered, "Now I lay me down to sleep, I pray the lord my soul to take, if I should die before I wake, I pray—I don't! Amen."

Mel whispered, "Amen!"

It seemed as if the lights had just gone off when they lit up the morning darkness like Times Square during the holidays. Bonnie headed to the showers while Mel made their beds. He had been to church camp many times, and this was very similar, he thought, waiting for Bonnie. He too needed to use the bathroom. He really had to pee before he could hit the showers.

It was not long before Mel and Bonnie had switched jobs and Bonnie sat combing her naturally curly head of hair, patiently waiting for Mel as he had done for her. Most of the people who had been in the shelter for the night had quietly moved on. The two of them were nearly starving. Taking their belongings, they got in a line that was clearly leading them to a nice, warm breakfast.

"Will you need a bag lunch?" they heard someone ask.They each answered with, "Thank you. Yes, please!" As they waited their turn in line, they thought about all the poor and hungry people in the world who did not have a place to sleep or shower, let alone a place where they handed out food to whoever came and stood in line.

Each taking a tray, silverware wrapped in a napkin, and a carton of milk, they walked down the line, where there was a choice of hot oatmeal, buttered toast, scrambled eggs, ham, and potatoes. At the very end of the line was a good selection of apples, oranges, and bananas looking somewhat beat up but nonetheless still very edible. Finding a good table to sit down at, Mel peeled a banana, revealing a most perfect tropical fruit. Slicing it on top of his oatmeal, he looked at the people eating their breakfast and b wed his head. Little Bonnie did the same. "Thank you, dear Lord, for this our daily bread, amen."

"Amen," little Bonnie repeated She proceeded to pour catsup all over her scrambled eggs. Little Bonnie laughed. "I just love scrambled eggs with ham smothered in tomato catsup, toast, and these little packets of strawberry jelly. It's totally perfect. I sure did sleep well last night. My bed was very comfortable. How did you sleep, Mister?"

Mel picked up a piece of little Bonnie's toast. When she stopped to take another dee breath, he stuck the piece of toast in her mouth. Mel gestured, pointing to his watch, and Bonnie knew what Mel was telling her. *Pretty basic,* she thought. *Eat my breakfast and shut up.*

Mel sat there enjoying his breakfast. *Ah,* he pondered, *so far so good.* Eating the last of his oatmeal, Mel wrapped his toast up in his napkin and stuck it in his vest pocket next to his bottled water. He had completely ignored Bonnie, who also was hiding an apple for later.

Mel got up and picked up his backpack. Bonnie did the same. Mel walked over to the lady handing out bag lunches, looked her directly in the eyes, and, taking one, said, "God bless you for helping so many good people, ma'am."

Bonnie, taking her bag, looked at the lady and said, "Have a nice day, ma'am."

Mel walked straight out to the street, turned right, and walked west down Main Street.

Bonnie, like a good assistant, just stayed a few steps behind him. Mel was like a bloodhound when he was on a scent. Bonnie liked Mel's uncanny ability to follow a trail no one else could see, including herself.

Standing in front of the public library, Mel waited for little Bonnie to catch up, as she had fallen behind a block or so back. Huffing and puffing, Bonnie walked right past Mel and walked up the library steps. Reaching the top, she took her apple out of her pocket and threw it at Mel. Mel ducked as the apple rolled out onto the street below. "Waste not, want not," he said as he shook his finger at Bonnie.

Bonnie yelled up at Mel standing at the top of the library steps, "I am glad I did not hit you in the head, Mel P. Dread. You don't need any more traumas done to that head of yours." She laughed.

As they sat at the top of the stairs waiting for the library to open at nine, Mel had time to give little Bonnie his instructions. "Listen to me," Mel said. "I need you to not talk while we are in the library. We will communicate by writing notes. If I hand you a note, please read it and do your best to be my assistant and do what it says. Do you think you can do that?"

Nodding, she said, "Don't be silly, Mel P. Dread. I am not a child, after all. Lead the way."

They could hear the library doors being unlocked. Mel looked at his watch. It was 9:00 a.m. sharp. Bonnie, holding the door open, repeated, "I said lead the way. You never hear anything I say, do you, Mel?"

Mel pointing to a sign that said, "Please be quiet!" Bonnie closed her mouth and followed Mel, walking past long wooden tables several long rows of labeled shelves. Mel seemed to know what he was looking for. Turning down a long row of books, Bonnie stopped and read the sign at the end of the row of books. In bold printed letters she read, "Des Moines City, History, Maps, Newspapers, Miscellaneous Rumors, Quips, Folklore, etc."

Mel took out his notebook from his backpack. Bonnie was amazed to see that Mel had obviously done hours of research. Mel looked prepared as he quickly began pulling out books and handing them to Bonnie. When the pile became just too big for Bonnie to handle, he took half the books from her. They walked over to a big wooden table and quietly laid the books down.

Pulling out a chair, Bonnie sat down. Pulling out his note pad, Mel wrote, "Help me look for anything about 149 Main Street, the number 457, Territorial bank, cemeteries, lost treasures, gold coins from 1855, or anything else you can find of interest," he wrote, handing the note to Bonnie.

Mel could not believe how quickly the time was passing. Bonnie was on her fourth book. He could see now why, as silly and as scatterbrained as Little Bonnie could be at times, she was very smart. She was a straight-A student at her school.

Both Mel and little Bonnie took notes for most of the morning and well into the afternoon. They nibbled steadily on pieces of their peanut and jelly sandwiches, salted pretzels, three chocolate Kisses, and juice pouches. Leaving all the books on the table, they both knew without saying a word that a nap in the park would do them both good after their long day. After gathering up their notes and cleaning up the big table as best they could, they went out the door and headed north on Sixth Street.

CHAPTER 4

Digging for Dread People or I Thought They Buried People Deeper Than That

"I assume you know where you are going," Bonnie said as she tried to keep up to Mel's longer legs. Mel knew that sometimes the less Bonnie knew the better, as she could get excited over the littlest of things. He knew that if he told her he was going to a cemetery to look for old gravestones, she would start asking all kinds of questions to which he had very few answers. So when Bonnie saw the street sign that read, "Woodland Cemetery, 7:00 a.m.–9:00 p.m." posted on the big wrought-iron gates of their destination, Mel took little Bonnie's hand and asked, "Are you afraid of cemeteries?"

"Afraid of cemeteries?" she laughed. "Me afraid of some big old cemetery full of dead people roaming around day after day night after night? Hell, yes," little Bonnie said, slapping Mel alongside his head. She then added, taking a moment to regain her composure, "Whatever. As long as there is daylight I will be fine, but you will never get me to come here after dark. Do you hear me, Mel P. Dread?" She ran to catch up to Mel.

Mel and Bonnie walked up and down each row of gravestones. As they walked by each grave marker, Mel would quickly scan the names with his eyes and move on to the next one. It was getting late, and they would soon have to head back to the mission, especially if they had to eat supper before seven.

Bonnie was wandering around, keeping close to Mel, when he heard her yell, "Hey Mel, come take a look at this!" As he ran over to where little Bonnie was standing, he could see a gigantic gravestone. He could not believe his eyes. It was the very same gravestone he had dreamed about. Hand-chiseled in the large granite rock was "Melvin Porter Dread, 1822–1902, Husband and Father. Bonnie Lou Dread, 1822–1902, Wife and Mother." Below their names was written, "God loves the rich as well as the poor."

Mel looked at Bonnie and said, "This is what I was looking for, Bonnie, and you found it. You found just what I was looking for, and I did not even tell you what I was looking for!" Mel laughed with joy. "I had better be careful or I will find myself being your assistant." He gave little Bonnie a hug. Little Bonnie hugged him back, only harder. She was glad to make Mel proud of her.

Bonnie stared at the names chiseled in the gravestone, perplexed. "Are these people related to you, Mel?" she asked impatiently. "Yes," Mel answered. "This is my great-grandfather, Melvin Porter Dread. Bonnie was his childhood sweetheart. They were married in 1842. They were married for sixty years, and they had two children: a daughter they named Elizabeth Ann and a son, Melvin Porter Dread II.

Mel looked at his watch and then at Bonnie. He said, "We have just enough time to get back to the mission. If we leave now, we will get back in time for a nice meal and a hot shower before bed, but we must hurry."

Slipping back through the wrought-iron gates, they headed for 600 Sixth Street. In less than twenty-five minutes, they were standing in line waiting for supper. With their trays in hand, they wondered what tonight's meal would be. Whatever it was, it smelled really good.

Soon they were eating fried chicken, mashed potatoes and gravy, cranberry sauce, and their choice of apple or banana cream pie. Most of the people had eaten already and had left to congregate in the parks, smoking their cigarettes and drinking from the liquor and wine bottles they had hidden in the park bushes earlier in the day. Many were waiting for the shelter doors to open. Other people just meandered in all different directions to spend their night somewhere other than the mission.

Bonnie had listened and did not say a word. Finishing her piece of banana cream pie, she began digging into Mel's slice of apple pie. When he had finished explaining the Dread family tree to her, Bonnie looked at Mel, totally perplexed, and said, "What do you think this all means, Mel?"

Mel said, "Please try to be patient, Bonnie. Solving any good mystery takes time! Besides, if it were that simple, my dear, relatively new best friend and assistant, do you not think someone would have solved the mystery and found the treasure by now?"

Mel looked at his watch. It was almost 8:00 p.m. when they arrived at the shelter door. There stood Mary Ann Leslie Claire, happy as could be to see them. She said, "I've been waiting for you two!" She motioned them inside and closed the big wooden doors behind them.

Mel thought to himself, *Tomorrow back to the cemetery, this time with a shovel.* He unconsciously spoke loudly enough for Bonnie to hear.

"Mel, did I just hear you say something ab ut finding a shovel?"

Bonnie asked sharply. "Tell me, Mr. Mel P. Dread IV, what are you planning on digging up? It had better not be any of those dead Dread relatives of yours, because you know, Mel, I have never really gotten into digging up Dread people—I mean, dead people. Are you listening to me?" Mel just lay on his cot, pretending to be asleep.

CHAPTER 5

Money in the Bank or Is There a Penalty for Early Withdrawal?

It was damp and sprinkling outside when the two of them finished eating their breakfast. Leaving the mission with their bag lunches, backpacks, and a good breakfast in their bellies, they set off walking north down Sixth Street. The sky was getting darker, and the wind was starting to blow out of the west.

Bonnie tugged on Mel's arm. "Mel, have you noticed that there is a massive black cloud above us? As your assistant, I feel I should advise you to find us shelter sooner than later."

Soon they were turning left on Grand Street. "Just a few more blocks," Mel told little Bonnie. He took her by the hand, and they both walked as fast as they could go. Lucky for them, the wind was at their backs. Big bolts of lightning were lighting up the dark sky all around them. Thunder boomed right above their heads as the rain and heavy hail began to pound. The streets looked as though they were beginning to flood.

Catching their breaths, they made it safely inside the Des Moines National Bank. There were only a few people in the bank, and more than likely they were either doing their banking or waiting for the rain to stop. Mel opened up his backpack and took out a large yellowed envelope. Then he proceeded to take out his picture ID from school, along with his authentic private eye card with a photo ID on it. Mel gave little Bonnie instructions to just sit there, watch their bags, and wait for him.

"Please, can you do that for me?" Mel asked.

Bonnie laughed. "Do you think, Mel P. Dread, that I am not smart enough to know when to come in out of the rain?"

Mel laughed back. "Of course you are. Now, just sit there and try to chill out for a few minutes, could you?"

Bonnie turned her head and crossed her legs. With her lips locked tight, she looked the other way. Mel turned and walked over to a big desk where a very thin lady was sitting. The lady had bright red hair. She was wearing black horn-rimmed glasses that sat low on her big nose. She wore a light green dress that matched her eye shadow. It looked as if her lips and eyebrows had been drawn on.

Mel said, "Excuse me, madam. I am in need of some assistance and wonder if you, kind lady, could help me?"

She looked at Mel and said, chuckling, "Why not? It's not like they close the bank because of the awful weather we are having. Now, how can I help you?"

First, Mel laid down his identification cards. The red-haired lady picked up his school ID and looked it over. Mel opened up the yellowing envelope and took out some papers. He handed the papers to the thin lady. She sat there studying what Mel had handed her. Mel went on to tell the lady that his grandfather had passed away, leaving everything to him. Before Mel's grandfather passed on, he had handed Mel this envelope with the papers inside. Mel gave the envelope to the lady to inspect for herself. Mel asked, "Do you know what these papers mean?"

"Well," the lady sitting in front of Mel said, "This number, this one here, seems to be a security box that may or may not be valid anymore." She went on to say that the old safe deposit boxes that were in this bank were given to the Des Moines City Historical Museum when the bank was remodeled. The nice lady wrote down the address, telling Mel it was not far away. She wrote "east on Grand Avenue" and scribbled a little map on the back of the yellow Post-it note, handing it to Mel.

Mel then pulled out a silver chain that was hanging around his neck. Mel showed the lady the small, tarnished key. She said, "Ah, yes. That could very much be a key to those old safe deposit boxes, but those boxes needed two keys. The first key unlocked the metal box, so it could be removed from the wall. A second key was needed to actually open the security box itself. You might go over to the Historical Museum to visit the exhibition on early banking in Des Moines. While you are there, you might try your key and find that you have one of the keys that will work, but don't forget, you're missing the second key." She chuckled. "Who knows? There may still be something in that old safe deposit box. Maybe a few old gold coins." The lady smiled at Mel and giggled.

Mel gathered up his papers and answered, "Ya never know. Ya just never know."

The storm had stopped, but the streets were running curbhigh with water, even though it had stopped raining. It did not look like a day that was going to see any sunshine, only gray, rainy skies. Mel walked over to Bonnie and said, "Mel P. Dread at your service.

May I take you to lunch, Bonnie Lou Starr?"

Bonnie said, "Yes, but only if you tell me what you're up to, Mel P. Dread. Do I need to remind you, we agreed we would share everything? Not even one little itty bitty secret," she demanded.

Mel replied, "Not a problem. Now, let's grab a chili dog and a cola, at which time I will fill you in on what I know and what I do not yet know."

"You're a good private eye, Mel P. Dread!" little Bonnie said, smiling at Mel.

"And you are the bes assistant a guy could ever hope for, Bonnie Lou Starr." Smiling, the two of them headed off to find chili dogs.

Other than the morning's bad weather, darn near everything else had gone smo thly. It was now Wednesday, and Mel knew they only had a couple more days before having to return to Ainsworth. They walked in the direction that the bank lady with the red hair had given them. They were trying to find the Des Moines Historical Museum.

Before long, they were in an old part of the city. There were old stores, shops, bakeries, and eateries here. Mel said, "Of all things." There was a man standing in front of a vintage cart reading, "Uncle Ed's Famous Chili Dogs."

When they walked up to the hot dog stand, the man tending stand said to Mel and little Bonnie, "Mornin', kids. Care to try one of my Uncle Ed's famous chili dogs?"

"How much?" Mel asked.

The man replied, "For you kids, a buck each, and for a second buck, I'll throw in two cold sodas."

Bonnie asked, excitedly, "Do you have Coke?"

Mel said, "Yes, a Coke for me as well, please, if you've got one, kind sir."

"That will be two Cokes and two of Uncle Ed's famous chili dogs, coming right up!"

Unzipping his backpack and digging deep into a big pocket, Mel dug out ten silver quarters. He paid the man and said, "You're a very kind man. We both thank you. Please keep the change."

The man handed them each a Coke and a chili dog wrapped up in tin foil more tightly than an Eskimo baby in winter. Uncle Ed pointed to a park bench across the street and said, "Bon appétit. Enjoy your day, and remember, God loves the poor as well as the rich. May God bless you both, always."

Crossing the street, Bonnie said, "Have you been counting how many times we've heard 'God loves the rich as much as he loves the poor?'"

Mel answered, "Yes, I have, and like you, Bonnie, it leaves me quite puzzled and a bit perplexed."

Removing their backpacks and setting them on the ground, they sat down on the park bench together. Opening her Coke and lifting the can, Bonnie made a toast. "Here's to me, here's to you, and here's to God, who I hope loves us when we are rich as well." Mel added, "And here's to finding lots of lost treasure!" The Coke cans clinked. Both taking a big chug, they began to unwrap the tin foil from their chili dogs. They savored every bite. Not a word was said as they finished consuming their Uncle Ed's famous chili dogs.

Mel finished his Coke and put his backpack on again, and little Bonnie did the same. Mel and Bonnie threw away the Coke cans and chili dog wrappers in the appropriate cans, which were clearly marked for recyclables or garbage only. Still without saying a word, Bonnie followed Mel, quietly thinking, *I love chili dogs. I could have eaten two!* Soon they were walking up the steps to the Des Moines Historical Museum. Mel held the door open as Bonnie entered. There was an older gentleman with white hair and big, bushy eyebrows standing next to a turnstile. The man said, "Welcome to the Des Moines Historical Museum. Please feel free to come on in and learn about the great history of our fine city. If you should have any questions, please feel free to ask any of the museum staff. Be sure you two visit our gift shop, located in our authentic historical street, which contains hundreds of historical artifacts."

Mel and Bonnie walked through the turnstile. Mel turned to the old man and asked him if there was an actual vault from one of the first banks in the city.

The old man answered, "Yes. You can walk right into the vault." The man added, "It's just like it was at the turn of the century. Well, just like it was, except that the gold that was in the vault is long gone." He chuckled. "Have fun, kids. We close at five p.m. on Wednesdays."

As the two of them strolled through the big museum, Mel thought about how there was so much history to learn about and so little time. Soon they were at the Main Street exhibit. It was an exact replica of a Des Moines street in the 1900s. Mel looked at Bonnie and said, "The bank. Let's find the bank."

It was not long before they were standing in front of the Iowa Territorial Bank of Des Moines exhibit. Walking inside, they were mesmerized by the big iron vault doors. Without saying a word, they walked into the vault. There, on one side, were rows after rows of metal security boxes. All had numbers and appeared locked, just as the thin lady at the bank had described. Mel could see two sets of locks. The lady was correct: two keys were needed, one to pull out the box and the second to open up the box itself.

Mel looked for the box that was numbered 457. Mel took out the key on the chain around his neck, stuck it in the first lock, and turned the key.

Bonnie squeaked, "Oh, sweet Jesus, God Almighty. You have one of the keys!"

Mel was frozen in time, lost in some sort of space continuum. His fingers could feel the key start to turn. As the key was slowly turning, he could feel his grandfather's presence in the room. Suddenly, there he was in Mel's mind's eye. His grandfather looked so happy, so healthy, and so young. Mel could see others, too. They all appeared to be healthy, happy, and young. Mel could see beams of light coming from his grandfather's eyes. Then when Mel's grandfather opened his mouth, a beam of light shot out of his mouth. It was as if lightning had struck him in the face. No words were uttered by either, but somewhere in that beam of light his grandfather was communicating with Mel.

Mel was frozen in that never-ending moment of time. His grandfather was communicating more information than he could possibly comprehend. What felt like hours actually happened in the time it took Mel to turn the key. Bonnie was still saying, "Jesus Christ Almighty, sweet Mother of God!"

When Mel pulled on the metal box, it came out just as it must have years ago. Mel gave it a bit of a shake and then shook it again a bit more aggressively. Suddenly they could hear a voice say, "Hey, Mom, check out this old bank."

Mel quickly replaced the metal box. He turned the key quickly to the left and pulled it out. Taking Bonnie's hand, Mel cocked his head, motioning for her to follow him out. They walked out of the bank and departed down the old cobblestone street, heading straight for the exit sign.

When they were standing outside again, Bonnie started asking Mel a thousand and one questions. Mel did not say a word   as little Bonnie kept on talking a mile a minute. After they had walked for about twenty minutes, Mel said, "Excuse me, dear assistant. Could you tell me what time it is?"

Bonnie looked at her watch and said, "It's 3:35."

"Perfect," Mel replied. "We have enough time to eat our bag lunches. And after we eat our lunch, Bonnie, I think we need to go back over to Woodland Cemetery and pull a few weeds from my great-grandfather's and great-grandmother's graves."

Bonnie said, as calmly as she could, "Mr. Mel P. Dread, am I not your assistant?"

Mel nodded his head.

"Did we not say we would share everything, information as well as treasure?"

Mel again nodded his head.

"You know darn well that after we eat our lunch," little Bonnie said, looking Mel directly in the eye, "the reason we are going back to that scary graveyard is to dig something up, Mr. Mel Porter Dread. As sure as I am standing here, we are not going back to pull weeds, plant, mow, or spit-polish that huge granite memorial to your great, great grandparents."

Mel, interrupting, said to little Bonnie, "They are my great-grandparents."

"Shut up," Bonnie said to Mel. "You know darn well you are taking me back there to dig up Dread people... I mean, dead people."

Mel replied, "You don't have to go, Bonnie."

She looked at him and said for the second time, "Shut up, Mel P. Dread. I have never been afraid of a little gardening. I love to pull weeds and spit-polish big granite gravestones."

Mel said, "Just relax, missy, and let's find a nice place to sit down and eat our lunch. I cannot wait to see what Mary Ann Leslie Claire's kitchen crew has made us for lunch today." Opening the lunch bags, they found their favorite: squashed peanut butter and jelly sandwiches. There was a bag of now completely crushed potato chips, along with a juice box and three candy Kisses.

Mel said to Bonnie, "Do you believe dead people can speak to the living?" as he took a big bite out of his sandwich.

"Mr. Mel P. Dread, do not tell me, Bonnie Lou Starr, that some of your private investigation skill comes from talking to dead people! Is that what you are going to tell me, Mel?"

Mel nodded his head yes and said, "It's true. I must confess I do indeed talk to Dread people."

Neither one of them said another word. They just finished their lunches and put on their backpacks. Then Mel got up and headed toward the Dread family grave plot, where Mel hoped that he could reap what his great-grandfather had already sown.

Opening the big wrought-iron gate, they headed directly over to the giant granite gravestone. Without missing a beat, Bonnie was on her knees, pulling weeds. Mel started to walk around the granite stone. After circling the gravestone several times, Mel dropped to his knees and began digging with his hands. Little Bonnie watched out of the corner of her eye while she kept pulling out weeds around the gravestone.

Mel took out his pocketknife and dug into the water-saturated soil. The digging was actually quite easy, easier than Mal would have imagined. He had a nice hole started, but he knew he must dig much deeper. His grandfather had always told him, "Mel, always remember, if you want to bury a treasure, always make sure it's buried below the frost line, or it won't stay buried." His grandpa would always then add, "The same holds true if you are digging for buried treasure."

Mel dug about twenty inches down into the soft soil. He had a hole about as big around as a basketball. Taking his knife, Mel poked it into the bottom of the hole, which was mostly sand. Before he could push it in very far, it hit what sounded like a rock. Bonnie, having pulled most of the weeds, started to take interest in the hole that Mel had dug. She stood up, looking over Mel's shoulder, and said, "I always thought they buried dead people deeper than that!"

Bonnie looked around. It was getting late. The dark clouds above looked as if they could burst at any time. Mel had uncovered what looked to be a flat rock, and it had a big X on it. It was just like the rock in the wall of the well where they had found the piggy bank with the three coins and a key to a locked security box on display at the Des Moines Historical Museum.

It was starting to rain. Mel was struggling to get the stone out of the hole. All of a sudden little Bonnie said, "Get out of my way, detective. Let a girl do it!" Mel needed a break, so he did not resist little Bonnie as she practically crawled into the hole headfirst. Bonnie began working to get her fingernails underneath two sides of the rock. With all her might, she started pulling up and down and shaking the rock. It was as if she were having a seizure.

Slowly Bonnie could feel the rock moving more and more. When Bonnie was sure it was loose, she backed out of the deep hole and said, "It's all yours, Dread." That was the first time that Bonnie had called Mel "Dread." Smiling at Mel with sand clinging to the upper half of her body, Bonnie motioned Mel to get back to the hole, saying to him, "I told you, Mel P. Dread, I was not digging up Dread people!"

Mel, with a little effort, pulled the flat rock out of the hole and sat it out of the way. Digging into the sand a few inches more, Mel uncovered what appeared to be some sort of fabric. Uncovering it more, he realized it was something wrapped in an old piece of cloth. Carefully removing the small cloth bundle, Mel handed it to Bonnie, who took it and laid it on the ground. She stepped back while Mel carefully unwrapped the cloth bundle.

While Mel was trying to loosen up the old cloth fabric, it felt as if what was inside the cloth had suddenly lost its shape! *Puzzling*, Mel thought to himself as he began to open the cloth. Bonnie was the first to say, "Oh my Gawd, it looks like another piggy bank. It looks just like the one we found down in the well." There were enough pieces to show them it had once been a piggy bank. Under some of the broken parts of the piggy bank lay three gold coins and a rusty old key. "Oh my Gawd, sweet Mother of Mary," Bonnie said, standing there in the rain, soaked.

They were both soaked and covered with dirt and sand. Mel, as quickly as he could, picked up the key and the gold coins. He quickly put them in his pants pocket. Rewrapping the broken pieces of the piggy bank, he placed the bundle back into the hole. Picking up the rock with the white X, he put it on top of the bundle of broken pig. Using their feet, little Bonnie and Mel soon managed to get all the sand they could back into the hole. Once again, Mel motioned to little Bonnie that it was time to go.

Looking at their watches, they saw that if they hurried they could still get a nice, hot meal, a warm shower, and a safe place to sleep. They made it back to the shelter in time to get in line for supper. The two of them were soaking wet and covered in sand. Mary Ann Leslie Claire, noticing them standing in line, walked over. As she went to say hello to Mel and little Bonnie, she hesitated, taking one good look at them both and muttering, "Oh my!" Mel, seeing Mary Ann Leslie Claire, said to her, "Good evening, good-looking. You're looking splendid as always."

Bonnie looked at Mary Ann Leslie Claire from head to toe and said, "Yes, you sure look nice and dry this evening, Ms. Saint Claire." "My name is Mary Ann Leslie Claire. There is no saint in my title yet," the woman said, giggling to herself. "You children enjoy your supper. The weather report says it is supposed to be a stormy night, so don't be late getting into the shelter. You would not want to have to sleep outside tonight." Mary Ann Leslie Claire continued to walk around, greeting others.

Bonnie had come to know Mel pretty well, and she knew he was deep in thought. The only thing to do was give him as much space as he needed, she thought as she ate her chicken-fried steak with mashed potatoes, covered in lots of catsup and gravy. So far the trip to Des Moines had been better than starring in a Walt Disney movie. She was daydreaming about the day when they would make a movie of her life. Bonnie took another gulp from her milk box and then wiped a trail of milk that was running down the corner of her mouth with her wet coat sleeve.

She smiled at Mel, looking him in the eyes rather like Betty Boop might have gazed into a man's eyes in one of her old cartoons. Little Bonnie leaned over and whispered to Mel, "I want you to always play my leading man, Mr. Mel Porter Dread."

Mel replied, "And you, my dear, shall always be my leading lady."

Bonnie, with catsup on both corners of her mouth, laughed. She was the happiest she had ever been! The lights went off sharply at the designated time. There were more people in the shelter tonight. Mel also noticed that there were a lot more children than on the last couple of nights. You could hear thunder and lightning outside. The rain was coming down hard, hitting against the big windows facing west, directly into the pelting summer storm. It was hot, humid, and just plain uncomfortable, making it impossible to sleep.

There were several ceiling fans buzzing overhead and a few big fans sitting on the floor that you could hear buzzing and whining. The fans had been placed around the perimeter of the gym. They seemed to keep the hot air in the big room moving around some. The wind and rain were both poundin relentlessly against the shelter's windows. The lightning bolts along with the thunder, were piercing and chilling to the bone. It was as nasty as any storm Mel could remember.

Bonnie, too, was hot. She was fanning herself with a religious pamphlet that someone had stuck under her pillow. Mel handed her his bottle of water. Little Bonnie took a big drink, passed it back to Mel, and whispered, "Thanks."

He took a drink and said, "You're welcome."

The sounds of children crying over at the other end of the room made it even more difficult to fall asleep. People had started to mill around, as it was too hot to lie on your bed and sweat. Bonnie and Mel were thinking along the same lines as they sat on the edges of their beds, peering into a dark room that was constantly being lit up by the sharp bolts of lightning. A loud crack from a lightning bolt once again startled the bajebees out of everyone who had taken refuge inside the shelter.

Mel whispered over to Bonnie, "It feels like it's the night of the living dead, don't you think?"

"Oh my Gawd, Mel," Bonnie answered him, "that's just what I was thinking! My goodness, Detective Dread, you must be reading my mind."

The time was passing like mold growing on an old piece of bread, and they wondered if the night would ever end. Somewhere in the late hours of the night, Mel and little Bonnie dozed off and managed to get a couple hours of sleep. Mel could see the sky outside through the high glass windows that faced to the west. The morning sky looked clear and was the color of the mourning dove's feathers: a soft gray-blue.

Bonnie, opening one of her eyes, looked over at Mel as he said to her, "Top of the morning to you, my little precious. How did you sleep?"

Bonnie, sitting up on the side of her cot, grabbed her head and answered Mel with, "Who are you, and how did you get in my hotel room?"

Mel answered, "Whoever does your hair deserves a big tip."

Most of Bonnie's hair was standing straight up in the air. The rest of her looked as though she had spent the entire night running away from flesh-eating zombies. Bonnie, slipping into her shoes, stood up, picked up her backpack, and, without uttering even one rhetorical comeback, walked away to take a shower.

Standing in the breakfast line, all they could smell were hotcakes and sausages. There would be plenty of time to enjoy their breakfast because the Historical Museum did not open until nine. Both Bonnie and Mel were wolfing down their hotcakes covered with pats of butter and lots of gluey, sugary syrup. They had two cartons of white milk, which they used to help wash their sticky hotcakes down their throats.

Mel said to Bonnie, "I need you to listen very carefully." Bonnie sat there while Mel told her of his plan to go back inside the Historical Museum's banking exhibit vault, taking the second key that they had found buried at the Woodland Cemetery.

Bonnie once again, without opening her mouth, managed to listen without even so much as a simple question. She stood up, picked up her bag, and said, "I got it. Thanks for sharing." Then she let out an unexpected loud belch and headed for the street. Bonnie loved it when she was the one in the lead.

Passing the counter, they each took a bag lunch. Mel said to the old man sitting there, "We thank you for your generosity and kindness." Bonnie, looking back, said, "Have a nice day." leaving Mel running to catch up to her.

Little Bonnie knew just how to get back to the Des Moines Historical Museum without any help from Mel. She was going to make it hard for Mel to keep up with her or die trying. Soon Mel was walking next to her. "Your backpack looks as though it has gotten lighter since yesterday, Bonnie Lou Starr," Mel said.

Bonnie replied, "I left all my dirty clothes in the hamper at the shelter—you know, the one they have in the showers for dirty towels." Opening the front door to the museum, she leaned over to Mel and said, "I hope you have not forgotten about our plans to be the richest twelve-year-olds in the world? In any case, Mr. Dread, we have a bank to rob. Are you coming or not?"

Having been behind the previous morning, Bonnie was leading the way this morning. "Good morning," Bonnie said to the old man standing inside the museum to greet them both. It was not the same older man as yesterday. This m n was short and was a bit overfed, as Bonnie's grandmother would often say about overweight individuals. His hands looked riddled with arthritis, but that did not stop him from introducing himself.

"Morning, folks. Welcome to the Des Moines Historical Museum. My name is Alfred "

Bonnie said, moving through the turnstile, "Good to meet you, Alfred. My name is Wendy, Wendy Wentworth, and this is my brother, Rodney Wentworth. We are in Des Moines visiting. We were here just the other day and had such a good time that we decided to return and spend a bit more time learning about the wonderful things Des Moines has to offer, especially to us younger folks. It's our youth that forms the hopes and dreams of this here great United States."

Mel was pushing Bonnie to just go. Mel said to the nice gentleman, "Excuse my sister. She tends to ramble on endlessly. You know how women are."

The man tugged at his toupee. It had slipped a little to one side.

Chuckling just a little bit, the old man replied to Mel, "My dear wife, God bless her soul, has been dead for more than three years now. I would give anything to hear her ramble on like women tend to do. You two live a long time and prosper." They walked out of his sight into the Historical Museum.

"Bonnie," Mel asked, "do you remember the plan?"

"Of course I do, Sherlock Holmes." Little Bonnie kept on walking, and before long they were both standing in front of the Iowa Territorial Bank Exhibit. Acting as if they were on a morning stroll through the museum, Bonnie stopped out in front of the bank. Little Bonnie would be playing the part of the lookout man. Mel felt as though he were Tom Cruise in the *Mission Impossible* movies. He entered the bank vault, took the key from around his neck, and stuck it into the first lock. Turning the key, he unlocked the box, releasing the inner box. Mel quickly pulled the security box out of the wall. Mel was already holding the second key between his lips. Laying the metal box on the counter, Mel inserted the second key.

He had trouble getting the old rusted key to turn. Mel pulled the second key out of the rusty lock and, quicker than lickety-split, spat a big, slimy blob of spit into the keyhole. Reinserting the second key, he tried turning it again. He could feel the key turning. The lock on the metal security box seemed to be unlocking, and suddenly the lock was open. Mel tugged on the lid, which opened with very little force.

Bonnie had been watching from outside the vault anxiously as Mel looked into the box. Bonnie was now peering over Mel's shoulder, standing on her tiptoes. She gasped. "Why, my goodness. That box appears to be empty!"

Mel picked the metal box up and turned it over, bottom side up. There stuck on the bottom of the box was what appeared to be an old, discolored postcard. Mel carefully removed the postcard. On the front of the postcard was an old picture of a farm. In the dim light of the vault it was too difficult to decipher what was written on the back.

Mel motioned and gave little Bonnie a gentle push. She went back over to her outpost in front of the vault. Mel, in no time at all, had locked the box and replaced it. He quickly walked out of the bank vault. He took Bonnie's hand as they headed for the museum exit. As they passed Alfred, who had dozed off to sleep, Bonnie said to him, "Live long and prosper." She thought to herself, however, that it would not be long before this old man joined his wife in the hereafter. Then he would once again be able to sit with his wife and listen to her nonstop chattering. The thought warmed little Bonnie's heart.

Bonnie was feeling as though they had been away from home for a long time now. Bonnie thought of her grandmother, her dead grandfather, and all those dead Dread people. Thinking about Dread people made little Bonnie laugh. Lost for a moment, little Bonnie had to race to catch up to Mel, who, unlike earlier in the day, was now ahead of her.

Little Bonnie wanted to get a better look at the postcard that Mel had found stuck on the bottom of the security box. She wondered if it might possibly be a map to the rest of the treasure.

Time was running out. Just one more day and they would be on the bus, heading back home to Ainsworth.

Finding a park bench, they both removed their backpacks and sat down. Mel took out his magnifying glass and held it over the postcard. It was old. On the front was a picture of what looked to be a horse pulling a plow, and there was a caption that read, "Come to Iowa, where the dirt is as good as gold." On the back side he could see it had been addressed to Mrs. Bonnie Lou Dread, 142 Main Street, Des Moines County, Illinois. The other side of the card was a hand-printed poem. Mel read it and handed it to little Bonnie, who also read it.

"Oh sweet mother of Mary, Mr. Mel P. Dread, what does this mean?"

Mel did not answer because he did not know.

Tomorrow they would catch the bus back to Nebraska, where they would again have to hitchhike back from Route 80, hoping at that point they would be lucky and not have any problems finding a ride north, back to Ainsworth. For now they would try to celebrate their last afternoon in the city of Des Moines Iowa by finding a place to get French fries and milkshakes. After they found the fries and shakes they would look for a good park bench. Where they could spend the rest of the day talking and enjoying each other's friendship! For soon it would be time for them to head back to the mission for their last night at the homeless shelter.

Mel lay awake on his cot and thought about the poem that was written on the back of this old postcard. Mel remembered the poem as if he had written it himself:

Three gold coins times two makes six,
Buried under rock and not under sticks,
You won't find it far from the center of town,
In a large room, where the holiness of holy bows down,
Somewhere a crucifix, Jesus hanging on the cross,
You will find something new, something old, something lost.

Mel kept recalling the address on the postcard. The card was postmarked 1908, and there was a penny stamp affixed to it. So Mel deduced that the postcard had been mailed. He also concluded that his great-grandfather was somehow part of something that Mel could not yet figure out. Thinking as a good private detective would, Mel asked himself who had actually seen the treasure. Who hid the treasure and why? There were few remaining records from the late 1800s, mostly rumors and some old folklore telling of a ton of old gold coins mysteriously vanishing, never to be found. Mel had so many questions and so few answers about all the puzzling information he had uncovered thus far.

The bus did not leave until 11:30 a.m. That would give Mel and Bonnie four hours to do more investigating. Mel still had the card and number of the cab driver who had picked them up four days earlier. The cab driver had told Mel not to think twice if they needed a ride. Mel would call him for their ride back to the bus station, for sure.

Bonnie was also lying on her cot, drifting in and out of sleep. She was randomly dreaming, and some of her thoughts were about having fun, laughing and playing while other parts of the dream were filled with fear. Bonnie rolled and turned. She was deep on one of her bad dreams. Sometime during the night, little Bonnie dreamed she was standing over a massive, black, bubbling tar pit. She was wearing a clown outfit. Her big, red nose was annoying her, and she kept pulling at it, but it would not come off. Bonnie rolled, tossed, turned, and pulled at her nose for most of the night, it seemed Then she dreamed that she was walking over the massive tar pit on a tightrope. She could see hundreds of people, some of whom she recognized. They were all staring up at her as she desperately tried to keep her balance on the taut high wire. Bonnie could hear the rat-tat-tat sound of a drummer tapping solo on his drum. Little Bonnie could see the excited faces of the crowd below her. Bonnie watched the crowd as their faces changed to expressions of horror.

Distracted by the faces of the people below, Bonnie suddenly lost her concentration, along with her balance. She had fallen off the wire and was in free fall. She heard screams from the people below as she felt herself falling, falling, falling. It seemed to go on for hours, and she thought that it might never end. Bonnie was tossing and turning, thrashing about. Mel was pulling on her arm, saying to her, "Wake up, Bonnie. Wake up."

Little Bonnie opened her eyes, and the first thing out of her mouth was, "Oh my Gawd, what time is it?"

Mel replied, "Gee, little Bonnie red nose, it's time for you to hit the showers. Get some breakfast, and try to have another great day."

It was Friday, and they still had a few hours before the six-hour bus ride toward home. Mel and Bonnie had jus finished eating big bowls of oatmeal when Mary Ann Leslie Claire appeared. Walking over to their table, she sat down with them. Exchanging good mornings, she said to them both, "Well, it certainly looks like it's going to be a nice, sunny day to travel."

Mel and Bonnie nodded their heads in agreement. Mel said, "We sure feel blessed to have been able to stay at such a wonderful shelter."

Bonnie added "It w s a godsend for us, for sure."

Mel remarked, "What a wonderful job Mary Ann Leslie Claire did of helping feed, c othe, and provide shelter for so many people who are in need of help."

Mary Ann Leslie Claire replied, "It's true. The cathedral and shelter have helped thousands of people who needed the church's compassion. But sometimes things must end. We can't always understand the workings of our Almighty Creator." She smiled at them both.

"What do you mean?" Mel asked.

She replied, "It costs more money than we have to keep the mission and shelter operating. By winter, when the shelter is most needed, I'm afraid our doors will be closed for good." Mary Ann Leslie Claire wiped tears from her eyes as she looked Mel and little Bonnie in the face. She said, "Every day I pray for a miracle from God, but unfortunately he has yet to hear my prayers."

Neither Bonnie nor Mel could think of anything to say, except, "We are so sorry, ma'am."

Mary Ann Leslie Claire stood up, wiping a few tears from her eyes, and asked them if they would like her to give them a personal tour of the Grand Cathedral. "The Grand Cathedral is where the holiest of holy bow down," she added. "It was finished after receiving a large donation from a private individual."

"Do you recall who donated all the money?" Mel asked. "Yes. It was a man named Dread," she said, adding that the family grave was just a few blocks away, in Woodland Cemetery.

She asked Mel if he had heard of the name "Dread," and Mel answered, "It sounds rather familiar."

Little Bonnie interrupted their conversation with, "I want to see where the holiest of holy bow down." Mel nodded his head in agreement.

Mary Ann Leslie Claire took Bonnie's hand and said to her, "Then you shall."

The cathedral was breathtaking. Everywhere you looked there was hand-carved statuary and art. The room made you feel small, unimportant, and inconsequential in comparison to its size and its beauty. Leading the way, Mary Ann Leslie Claire spoke about the church's history and some of the people who had come to pray in this very spot. Bonnie asked, "Is this was where the holiest of holy bowed down?"

"This is the place." In a saintly voice she said, "Shall we bow down and pray?"

All three of them kneeled to pray. Bonnie looked at the big statue they were kneeling in front of. Little Bonnie and Mel could not help but marvel at the statue. It depicted Jesus, nailed nearly naked to the burdensome, heavy, wooden cross. A thorny crown stuck on top of his head. Jesus was bleeding from his wounds. The blood looked as though it were actually dripping from his head and from the holes where the nails had pierced his flesh. Bonnie reached over to touch a drop of blood, which was on the floor where she was kneeling. Then she pulled her hand back quickly, thinking, *What if it were real blood?* Mary Ann Leslie Claire finished her prayer, and the three of them stood up. Bonnie and Mel, still staring at the impressive statue, acted starstruck. The light shining through the stained glass church windows surrounding the statue made the colorful, hand-painted image of Jesus seem to come alive. Mary Ann Leslie Claire, in a rather saintly voice, asked little Bonnie and Mel if they thought God really loved the poor people as well as the very rich. Mel answered, "Could you define love?"

Soon it was time for them to say good-bye, bringing an end to their stay at the Cathedral shelter. Mel and Bonnie waved so long and headed down the steps of the church with their backpacks in tow. Bonnie followed Mel west up Sixth Street. Seeing the phone booth, Mel reached into his pocket and took out one quarter and one dime. He put them in the slot and dialed the number on the card. After a couple of rings, the voice on the other end said, "Need a cab?"

Mel replied, "Yes, we do. My sister and I are at a phone booth on Sixth and Grand Avenue."

The voice on the other end said, "I'll be there in less than five minutes."

It had only been a few minutes when the cab pulled up. The cab driver recognized Mel and little Bonnie right away. He jumped out of the cab and opened both side doors for them. "Jump in," he said with a big grin on his face. "Well, I'll be damned. It sure is good to see you two once again. How has your week been here in Des Moines?" he inquired, closing the side doors and getting in the cab himself.

He asked Mel, "Where to, hotshot?"

"To the bus station," Mel replied. "We have a 12:45 bus to catch back to Ainsworth, Nebraska."

Mel began to answer the driver's question of how their week was by saying, "My real name is Mel, and this is my friend, Bonnie. We said we were here on business. The truth is, we were really here looking for lost treasure."

The driver, surprised by Mel's answer, said, "Mel, if you found some treasure, I'd say you just might be in the right business."

Bonnie, speaking loudly, remarked, "We've hardly found any treasure at all!"

Mel interrupted little Bonnie as soon as he could. "What Bonnie is trying to say is that we spent the week visiting the Des Moines Historical Museum. The wonderful lady who runs the shelter gave us a tour of the Grand Cathedral, where we saw a beautiful statue of Jesus. She made us feel right at home while we were at the shelter."

Mel thanked the cab driver for taking them to the shelter when they first arrived in Des Moines. "Your generosity and kindness will always be remembered."

It was not long before they were in front of the Route 80 bus station. Opening the doors and helping them with their backpacks, the cabby said, "No charge. Kids under twelve ride free."

Mel answered, "How can we ever repay you?"

The cabby said, "When you find that treasure you two are looking for and you have more money than Santa Claus has white hair, remember me." Smiling at them, he said, "What goes around always comes around."

Then he was in his cab and off to catch his next fare. Mel thought, *Unless you're rich, everyone has to earn their money somehow!* Mel had hoped he would find some answers while in Des Moines, and he had, but he did not know where the gold treasure was. Right now Mel did not have any plans except to get on the bus and head home to good old Ainsworth. When people started boarding the bus, Mel dug into his backpack and pulled out the return tickets. Then he and little Bonnie got in line. The few travelers quickly boarded the big bus, and soon the bus was pulling out onto Route 80. They were heading west toward Nebraska, in the direction that would eventually get them back home.

Bonnie asked Mel what he was thinking. Mel said, "Right now, nothing! I am going to try to chill out myself and enjoy the ride home." Bonnie closed her eyes and fell asleep. Mel could not relax. His mind was wound up tighter than a yo-yo at a yo-yo convention, so he spent the next few hours staring out the bus window and humming some of his favorite songs. Bonnie mostly slept.

The trip back seemed much longer than the trip out had. *It always seems that way,* thought Mel as they finally pulled into the stop along Route 80. That was where they needed to try to find a ride back to Ainsworth, some fifty or so miles north and a bit to the west. Standing by the side of the road, they patiently waited for a passing motorist to give them a ride.

CHAPTER 6

Playing Dread or We Got Some Splainin' to Do

There were not many cars or trucks going north, it seemed to them both, as they were passed by a van full of children. "No room," Bonnie commented. A semi truck hauling pigs drove by. "Too stinky," said Mel.

A motorcycle was coming up the road. "I could go on without you, Mel," Bonnie said, laughing.

It was starting to get dark. They could see the headlights of a car approaching. In desperation, Mel yelled, "Quick, Bonnie. Stand in the middle of the road. I will pretend to have been injured."

As Mel collapsed on the side of the road and played dead, Bonnie, as if trying out for the cheerleading squad, started jumping up and down, and throwing her arms around.

The car began to show down as Bonnie started yelling, "Please help us! Please help us!" The car pulled up alongside Bonnie, who by now had gained her composure. It was dark and the man in the car said, "My dear lord, little girl. What on earth is wrong?"

Bonnie calmly said, "My brother and I are trying to get back to Ainsworth, about fifty miles up the road from here, but my brother seems to have collapsed and I cannot wake him up."

The man pulled the car over to the side of the road and quickly got out of the car. He hurried over to the boy lying on the ground. Just as the man kneeled down, Mel opened his eyes and gasped. "Dad!"

Bonnie yelled, "Dad?" Dad yelled, "Mel?"

Mel reached his hand out to his father and for a lack of any other words said, "Why, hello, Dad. You mind giving me a hand getting off the ground?"

Mel, now back on his feet, said pointing, "So, Dad, do you remember my friend, Bonnie, from across the street?" In Mel's best Ricky Ricardo voice, he said, "Eeeeee, I am sure, Lucy and I, we got some splainin' to do."

His father, hearing Mel's bad Ricky Ricardo imitation, said, "Yes, as the Lord is my witness, you've both got a lot of splainin' to do."

Mel said, "I am sure, Dad, I can explain each and every question that you might have. Except, Dad, the problem is, Bonnie and I took an oath. We promised and hoped to die that we would never tell another soul about certain things, which I am not at liberty to discuss. Bottom line, Dad, we took a solemn oath, and we both swore on the Bible that we would rot in Hell if either of us blabbed and told another soul."

"You're both twelve years old. What does either of you know about rotting in Hell?" Mel's father asked.

"Well!" Mel thought about his father's question. Then he replied, "I think it kind of speaks for itself."

Bonnie, nodding her head in agreement with Mel, finally decided to speak up and said, "We're not little kids anymore, Pastor Dread. We know it's Hell when dead stuff starts to rot!"

Mel's father, although very angry, calmly said to Mel, "Nothing surprises me anymore about your behavior. Now, both of you get in the car. I can see that your bad behavior is partly my fault. Mel! You are so much more independent than most kids your age. You always have been just too damn independent! I expect you get it from your grandfather. I remember him telling me so many stories when I was a young boy about all his wild adventures as he turned into a strapping young man."

"What kind of stories?" Mel asked. "Anything about lost treasure, gold coins, mystery, suspense, drama, dead people?"

"Dead people?" His father laughed. "I assume that your grandfather might have told you some of his old stories."

Mel said, "Dad, I went to live with my grandfather because no one else did. Grandpa was full of long conversations; I could not understand most of them. You know, Grandpa had dementia, and he often did not seem to make any sense to me. I was not even nine years old; there was so much I did not understand. All I know is that my Grandpa loved me, and I loved him. The rest I am trying to figure out on my own."

His father knew Mel had grown up years before his time, and for that he was sorry. Pastor Dread had always prayed to God for forgiveness. He was sorry he had made so many mistakes in his life. He knew, in spite of it all, that he and Mel were trying to do the very best they could. For that, Pastor Dread was very thankful! He was also thankful that whatever Mel had been doing fifty miles from home, he was now safe. Why was Mel, the son of a pastor, on the side of the highway with a girl who was in Ainsworth spending the summer with her grandmother? All Pastor Dread really knew was that her name was Bonnie and she lived directly across the street from his son. He felt thankful that they were both home safe w th no apparent damage done. Soon after he pulled into the driveway and turned off the car the three of them were inside the house, where Mel's dad asked "as a welcome home celebration, how about I order the three of us a large pizza? In thirty minutes or less, we can be eating pizza, after which you, my dear son, can feel free to ask me any questions you would like. I will, of course, do my best to honestly tell you what I know."

Mel said, "Pizza? Yee haw! Order me a large Coke, too, Dad." Mel ran up the stairs to jump in the shower. He was excited to ask his dad some questions that would help Mel in his investigation of the Dread family riddle.

Detective Mel P. Dread would get to interrogate his father with lots of questions He would be very careful not to let his father know anything that he already knew. Mel had no plans to tell his father about his having already dug up the two piggy banks. Nor could he tell anyone he had found keys that opened a metal security box in the city of Des Moines, that his detective work had led him to the old postcard taped to the bottom of the box, or that the postcard had an address and a strange poem written on the back. He could not tell his father that he had possession of six gold coins, that he had visited his great-grandfather's grave in Iowa, or that he, along with Bonnie, had dug up that second piggy bank at the Dread family cemetery plot. Mel knew that it also meant he would never let his dad know that he and little Bonnie had spent nearly a week in a homeless shelter in downtown Des Moines, Iowa. Until he was good and ready, just little Bonnie and her boss, detective Mel Porter Dread, could know!

Keeping the cat in the bag should be easy for a master detective like him—at least, so Mel hoped.

Mel heard the doorbell ring. He bounded down the steps in just his boxer shorts, yelling, "Pizza's here, Dad. Do you have some cash, or are you paying him with a credit card?"

Mel answered the door. There stood the pizza guy, holding their pizza and two colas.

"Good evening," the delivery man said happily. "That will be $18.53." The delivery man was wearing a red baseball cap and matching red shirt. The cap, the shirt, and the pizza box said, "Pig out Pizza."

Mel's dad handed him a twenty-dollar bill and said, "You keep the change."

"Enjoy your pizza," the delivery boy said as he imitated a snorting pig and loudly proclaimed, "Pig out Pizza rules!"

Closing the door, Mel said to Bonnie and his dad, "Did you see the pizza guy's tattoo? It was a tattoo of a fat little pig."

"No, I did not notice his tatto . Why, son?" Mel's father asked. "Don't tell me you're going to be one of those people who starts out wanting just one little tattoo. By the time you get to be twenty-five years old, you would not only be covered in body ink but would wish you had listened to me and not gotten any" Mel replied, "Hindsight is 20/20, isn't it, Dad?" Mel made a pig sound like the delivery boy had made and said, "Come on, Dad, let's pig out."

Picking up a big, juicy piece of pizza, Mel stuck it in his mouth. His taste buds were screaming "Bravo, bravo," and crying out in extreme happiness as he savored his first bite of his pizza.

As Mel's dad was popping open their cans of soda, he said, "Please, Mel, no tattoos until you're at much older and much wiser!" Mel's face glazed over. He could not believe that his father, the pastor of the local church, had actually said that his son, Mel P. Dread, could get a tattoo when he reached the age of fifteen. "Thank God from whom all blessings flow" popped quickly into Mel's mind. Mel nodded his head with his mouth full of pizza and mumbled, "No tattoos until I am at least fifteen. I promise!"

*   *   *

"I cannot believe we actually finished a large pizza. Can you, Melvin Perfect Dread IV?"

"It was a really good pizza," Mel exclaimed to his father. Bonnie had fallen asleep in an old, overstuffed chair, totally oblivious to her surroundings.

Mel's first question to his dad was, "How come I, too, was named Melvin Porter Dread?"

"Well, Mel," his father said, "When you were born, your mother and I could not agree on a name for you. It had been nearly three months after your birth, and we still had no a name for you That's when we were told we either had to give you a name or the County Records Office would write 'John Doe Dread' as your birth name."

Mel laughed. "John Doe Dread. So wh t did you do?"

"Well, son, since your great-grandfather was named Melvin P. Dread, your grandfather's name was Melvin P. Dread, and my name is Melvin P. Dread, son, your name is Melvin P. Dread."

Mel asked, "Why were all of us named Melvin Porter Dread, Dad?"

"It all started back in a rural Iowa farm, not far from what is now Des Moines. It is rumored, that your great-grandfather, as a young man, found a ton or so of gold, which he went to great measures to hide. No one knows where he hid the ton of gold, and to this day it has never been found. Every generation since then named their first son Melvin Porter Dread, which would make any of us Dread men rightful owners of the lost gold, if it were ever found."

"That is amazing, just amazing!" Mel exclaimed. "Why, Dad, was I never told about such an incredible part of my family history?" His father, looking deep into his son Mel's eyes with the most serious expression on his face, answered, "Because, Melvin Porter Dread IV, looking for lost treasure will drive you insane!"

Mel sat for the next few hours, listening to his father telling him stories about things he had never spoken of before. Maybe Mel thought that his father had filled up his life with the church, with reading, memorizing scriptures, and studying to become a preacher, after his mom left them both. Mel's mom had left them shortly after Mel's third birthday. He could not remember her, or maybe he just chose not to!

It might be, Mel thought, that that a person's life turns out the way it was supposed to—or maybe life turns out the way it does because somewhere along the line people just give up. We just give up, and eventually we all die, leaving all our dreams for someone else. In death there is so much unfinished business. With life there is hope, and Mel was more hopeful than ever.

Mel had been able to have his father answer so many of his questions. Mel now knew that Melvin Porter Dread I, his great-grandfather, had lived in Des Moines, Iowa, around the turn of the century. At a very young age, Mel's great-grandfather started working with the stonemasons who worked on the famous Des Moines Christian Cathedral. By the time he was fifteen, he was a master mason. Much of the ornateness and the architectural art throughout the cathedral were actually worked on by his great-grandfather.

When he reached his twenty-first birthday, Mel's great-grand-father married Mel's great-grandmother, Bonnie Lou Brody, who was the love of his life. Mel also learned that Bonnie Lou was two months pregnant when they were married. His great-grandmother gave birth to a premature baby girl six months later. That girl was followed by her new baby brother, who eventually would turn out to be Mel's grandfather and the father of Mel's dad.

His great-grandfather was a truly religious man and became an ordained minister. He eventually became a minister at the Des Moines Cathedral, the very cathedral he had worked on for many years on as a young mason. The church was his great-grandfather's life for the next thirty years until his death.

It was very late. Mel's father went to bed, and Mel was quickly falling asleep on the couch. He knew he would see Bonnie tomorrow morning in church. Mel was anxious to tell her about the conversations he had with his father. Mel had lots of splainin' to do, and he knew it would all have to wait until after church.

Mel and his father both overslept on that particular Sunday morning. Waking up late, Mel's father ran around like a chicken with its head cut off, gathering all the things he would need to give his sermon. Running out the door, dragging his suit coat and his necktie, he yelled loudly, "Mel, get up! Get up, Mel! You had better get up, Mel. You're going to be late for church!"

Mel did not hear the door close or his father's car pull out of the driveway. Mel was fast asleep, totally dead to the world. This was one Sunday morning sermon his father would be making to everyone else but Mel.

Not So Very Long Ago or This Statue Looks Vaguely Familiar

Startled, Mel quickly sat up to a voice whispering, "Mel… Detective Mel Porter Dread… wake up!"

Mel's head was still fuzzy from not having slept well all night on the living room couch. With his eyes wide open, Mel could Bonnie standing there staring at Mel in his boxer shorts, with his hair looking like he had been in a windstorm. Bonnie was talking a mile a minute. "All I can think about," she said, "is everything I think I know, stacked up against all the stuff that I am clueless about. I still do not have an inkling of how you plan to ever find any gold treasure." Bonnie looked at Mel, taking a deep breath.

It was Mel's chance to interrupt Bonnie, as he so often had to do. "Settle down, missy. I understand your frustrations." In his best Ricky Ricardo voice, he said, "Listen up. I got some splainin' to do, so please pay attention!"

Suddenly the front door swung open, and in walked two church ladies followed closely by Pastor Dread. The ladies, who were carrying two trays of food, were met by the sight of little Bonnie standing next to Mel, who was still in his boxer shorts. Everyone was looking at Mel and little Bonnie standing next to him, speechless. Mel, as usual taking charge of this awkward situation, said politely, as he tried to pat down his hair down and make himself look somewhat presentable, "Welcome to the Dread family home. Can I—I mean, can we give you a hand with those heavy trays?"

He pushed Bonnie over to take a tray and took the second tray from the other lady's hands. With the food trays in hand, the two quickly darted into the kitchen without another word.

Mel's dad said, "It's nothing to be concerned about, ladies. My son was a little under the weather this morning, and he had my permission to miss church."

"We pray to our good Lord above to help your son get to feeling better very soon," said the larger of the two women as Pastor Dread kindly asked the two ladies to sit down on the sofa.

"Shall I make us a cup of tea and then we can talk about finding a qualified pastor to replace me?" As Pastor Dread politely excused himself, he walked into the kitchen to prepare some tea. He heard the ladies talking in the living room, saying something about how it would be hard to replace such a wonderful man as Pastor Dread. Big tears rolled down the pastor's cheek.

It was not long before he reappeared with a tray of cookies, a bowl of sugar, some creamer, and some hand-stitched napkins. Then he went back for the teapot full of hot, steaming Earl Grey tea. Returning, Pastor Dread poured tea into three cups, sat down, and asked, "Which one of you wonderful ladies made these cookies?" He dipped a cookie into his cup of Earl Grey tea.

The smaller of the two ladies winked at Pastor Dread as she took hold of the pastor's hand and said, "You're a wonderful man, Pastor Dread. You must get very lonely at night." Both the lovely ladies smiled at Pastor Dread.

Wide-eyed Pastor Dread bowed his head, saying, "Shall we pray, dear ladies? Dear Lord, as we try to forget those sometimes lustful, earthly needs that God has placed in front of us all to test our faith, we ask for God's forgiveness. May He make us strong in order to resist the temptations of the flesh." He finished with, "Amen!"

Smiling at the two ladies, he asked, "Would you dear ladies care for some more tea?" They both smiled pretentiously at Pastor Dread.

"No," they both said, simultaneously. "It's time for us to go." The two ladies got up and left, never once mentioning Pastor Dread's replacement.

Mel had been across the street sitting on Bonnie's grandmother's porch, with Bonnie sitting by his side. They both watched as Sara Lee and her sister Sara Jean left Mel's house and walked to their car and drove away.

"Those two women have never been married," Mel said. "Those bothersome women are always flirting with my dad!"

Bonnie said, "Well, I would suppose that they are both old and lonely. Let's face it. Your dad would make a fine husband for some nice middle-aged woman."

Mel, laughing, said, "Please, God, I don't want Sara Jean Barnhart or Sara Lee Barnhart as my stepmother!" Laughing again, Mel said, "Besides, I think my dad is committed to remaining a single man of the cloth. I think maybe that is why my mother left my dad. I think it is also why he joined the church!"

"So," Bonnie asked, "Do you think your father would ever settle down with a nice lady if he found one?" Mel, after a moment of thought, answered with, "Well, my dad divorced my mom when I was three years old, and ever since then he has been married to the church, it would seem."

"Well," little Bonnie said, "I think you're dead wrong. But there is only so much information one little girl can take in while visiting her elderly grandmother in Ainsworth, Nebraska."

Mel said, "I am a very good detective, so I am always listening, watching, and gathering information. Do not forget that I was born with a mind that seems to remember nearly everything that I have experienced. It's an awful lot for a twelve-year-old boy to think about. So all I can do is try to put everything that's floating around inside my head into the correct scenario. I have been trying my best to put every piece of the puzzle into the equation." "Then what?" Bonnie asked Mel, with a bit too much skepticism. "Then, just like magic," Mel answered, "one day all the pieces will come together. Bonnie Lou Starr, we may eventually be very surprised to find that the gold has always been right in front of everyone's eyes!" "That's poetic and most reassuring for me," little Bonnie told Mel.

"I have just one thing to say to you, Detective Mel P. Dread IV." In a loud voice, little Bonnie hollered out, "Show me the money! Show me the treasure! Show me a treasure map, Mel."

Then little Bonnie added, "It's clear to me that you and I have reached another Dread end. I guess that means no soup for us!" She laughed.

"I am beginning to think that God does love us poor as he does those who have money," Bonnie's best friend, Mel, declared without many reservations.

"Good thing," she added, "because we are both poor, it would seem." Mel said, "Please remain patient, my dear little Bonnie.

Haven't you heard that God works in mysterious ways?"

"To you, Mel Porter Dread, everything is a mystery that you feel a need to solve. So, how can I assist you in finding the one thing we agreed to find, your great-grandfather's treasure, the treasure we agreed we would split fifty-fifty?"

Mel adamantly demanded to know what little Bonnie thought they both had been working on all this time. "After all, Bonnie, the treasure has been missing for over a hundred years, and I think it's time someone solved the Mel P. Dread family mystery. All I need to do is figure out where my great-grandfather, Mel P. Dread I, would have hidden more than a ton of gold coins."

Bonnie asked Mel, "Do you really think you have what it takes to solve a hundred-year-old mystery, a mystery involving a ton of missing gold coins?"

"Not at this moment," Mel answered, "but with a few more missing pieces of the puzzle, we just might find the gold has been in front of everybody all along."

"Do you think those missing pieces have anything to do with that strange poem on the back of the old postcard?" little Bonnie asked. "Why do you think someone would have taped that old postcard on the bottom of an old security box unless it meant there was really a treasure hidden somewhere?"

Mel replied, "Exactly. That is exactly what I believe also, Bonnie. You're a pretty smart cookie when you want to be, Bonnie Lou Starr." Bonnie smiled at Mel.

Mel needed a few more pieces of the missing puzzle. He went online and typed in the words "history of Des Moines National Cathedral church." Up popped over forty-five different websites about the Des Moines Cathedral's early history. Scanning the list, Mel clicked on a description of the early stone and casting techniques which were used in building the cathedral.

According to one site, the church was home to many arts and treasures. The word "treasure" caught Mel's eye. Soon he was looking at some amazing old pictures of men working at building the early Des Moines Cathedral. The pictures were in black and white but were amazingly clear. There was so much information about masonry techniques, about the workers, and about those artists who carved or cast the statues and artworks that were now placed in the Cathedral.

The information about cement and plaster casting fascinated Mel very much. He spent the next couple of hours reading about the techniques that the masons used in making the cathedral into the magnificent architectural marvel it was. Much of the interior art and statues were cast in plaster or concrete. Then hand-painted fresco was applied. Coat after coat of patinas and hand painting would finish the detailed artwork. The frescos were exquisite and were applied to every surface.

Mel found a picture of a large statue with a young man beside it. Under the photo was a caption that read, "A rare picture of the yet uncompleted statue of Jesus Christ which was cast for the Des Moines Cathedral's main sanctuary. The statue was intended to be a place where holy men would bow down and receive communion." There were many more pictures of the statue in progress. The last picture was of the finished statue. It was the very same statue that Mary Ann Leslie Claire had shown them.

Mel zoomed in on one of the black and white photos. There stood a young man whom Mel thought to be his great-grandfather, Mel P. Dread I. Mel printed out the photograph for his records.

Mel kept reading until he could not keep his eyes open any longer. Bookmarking the important websites, he turned off his computer and then flicked off the overhead bedroom light. Mel crawled into his bed and drifted into a state of unconsciousness.

Mel had more questions that he needed to ask his father. One was, where did the art work in the Ainsworth Church come from? Mel thought it looked curiously like the statues and artwork from the Des Moines Cathedral.

Mel thought about the poem on the old postcard. He knew that in the poem lay the answer to this mystery of the lost gold. Mel pulled out the old postcard and stared at what had been written on the card, which had been postmarked 1905.

"Three gold coins times two makes six," Mel thought to himself. They had found two sets of three gold coins, adding up to six. The next line was, "It's buried under rock, not under sticks." Both piggy banks were covered by rocks with big X's painted on them. "You won't find it far from the center of town." He thought, *The church is always the center of any new community, especially back in the late 1800s and early 1900s.*

"In a room where the holiest of holy bow down" could only be referring to the place in the cathedral that Mary Ann Leslie Claire had shown them.

"Somewhere a crucifix of Jesus hanging on a cross." Mel was confused by that line. Mel read the last line: "You will find something new, something old and something lost." Mel thought again about the statue of Jesus. The statue was covered with handpainted fresco, which was simply paint mixed with plaster. Mel remembered how it was beautifully painted and how it sparkled as if there were gold specks mixed into the patina. Although the statue in Mel's church was smaller in size, it looked just lik a copy of the statue in the Des Moines Cathedral, as far as Mel could tell. But before he could deduce any more, Mel fell fast asleep.

Morning was just a few long hours away, and Mel's mind wandered all night long. Dreaming again, Mel could see himself walking down a path, holding his grandfather's hand. His grandfather had bright light shooting out of his eyes and his mouth.

When Mel looked into his grandfather's eyes, he could hear him say, "God loves the poor as well as the rich, Melvin Porter Dread. You have done well, my grandchild. You have made all us Dreads very proud of you, proud of you, proud of you."

Waking up, Mel could see the sun shining through his bedroom window. Jumping out of bed, Mel quickly took his morning shower and ate some breakfast. Then it was time to talk to his dad. Mel needed some more family history, and he believed his father would be able to tell him what he needed to know. He headed to the study, where he knew he would find his father reading his Bible. "Morning, Dad," Mel said to his father, who was sitting quietly and studying his Bible.

"Morning, Son. What's on your mind?" It was rare for Mel to come into his father's study this early in the morning to chit-chat. "I have a couple more questions I thought you might help me with." "Okay, Son. Shoot away with your questions," his father said, laying his Bible down.

"First, Dad, where did the statues and artwork in our church come from?" Mel told his father he had gone online and had been looking at websites about the Des Moines Cathedral, which his great-grandfather had helped to build around 1893. The church and all of the art at the Des

Moines Cathedral had been built by masons and artisans, one of whom was Mel's great-grandfather.

Mel asked his father, "Is it true?" Mel's dad nodded.

"Well, Dad, did any of the art or statues in our church ever come from Des Moines, Iowa?"

"My father used to tell me about his father, my grandfather, your great-grandfather, giving our church here in Ainsworth many of its religious artworks. That was when your grandfather, my father, was presiding over the very same church that we both still attend each Sunday here in Ainsworth, Nebraska."

"Wow,"Mel exclaimed."What are the chances of that happening?" "Well, Mel, we all know that truth is better than fiction! The church we have here in Ainsworth was an outreach mission built back about 1912. The Christian Temple Cathedral would often send masons and artisans to help construct and work on what was then known as the Ainsworth territorial church."

"Dad," Mel asked his father, "do you believe in any of the Melvin P. Dread folklore—you know, about lost gold treasure, hidden but never found? Because, Dad, I believe…"

"Melvin," his father sharply interrupted, "if I told you that I did believe, it could do neither of us any good. Just remember, son: money, riches, and wealth are the devil's tools. Don't you start chasing after all that family folklore, believing that talk about gold and lost treasure maps. None of us Dreads have succeeded in finding that treasure, and believe me, son, we have all tried!"

Mel could not believe what he was hearing. "You mean, Dad, you have tried to discover what I now am hoping to find, the Dread family fortune?"

"Yes, Mel. Over one ton of gold coins disappeared, and the gold was never seen again. Mel, I beg of you, do not waste more time chasing the devil's gold. That's why the entire Dread family swore years ago to never mention the lost gold coins again. I am not sure why I have engaged in all these silly conversations about lost treasure. How many times do I have to preach to you about how God loves us poor as well as those who are rich?"

Mel thought that his dad, the preacher, was trying to convince himself of his words. Mel did not believe that was how his father really felt.

"Listen, Son, how about I make plans for us to go to Des Moines, Iowa? I have business there for two days next week. You and I could visit the cathedral that Melvin P. Dread helped to build well over one hundred years ago. I have several meetings with other church representatives who also will be there visiting. It will just be for one night, so it is no big deal. What do you think, son?" Mel's father asked. "Hey, maybe your friend, Bonnie, would like to come too? I mean, providing her grandmother would allow her to tag along. I will go over tomorrow and speak to Bonnie's grandmother directly."

"Gee, Dad that would be great. I know how I would surely be excited to finally ge to visit Des Moines and see the cathedral up close.

I have seen many pictures on my computer of the early stages in its building and how so much of the ornate artwork was achieved." Mel stood up. "Dad, can I be excused to go inform little Bonnie we are going to visit Des Moines, Iowa? Of course, provided her grandmother says it's okay."

Ringing the doorbell, Mel waited for little Bonnie to come running and open the door. He rang it again and again, hoping to see the face of his friend, but no one came to the door. Mel sat down on their front porch. He felt like he had not talked to his best friend in so long. He was happy, he was sad, and he was very anxious to talk to little Bonnie about the opportunity that he thought would be priceless. Mel waited for an hour or more, but there was no sign of Bonnie or her grandmother.

Mel walked home, hoping everything was all right at his bestfriend's house. Although Mel felt deep in his stomach that something had happened, he prayed that everything would be okay. Mel could only go home and make his plans to return to Des Moines, Iowa, where he would get a second chance to look for that one ton of gold coins that no one else had been able to find.

Mel was sure his dad was right. Looking for lost treasure might drive a person crazy, but finding the treasure would also make him very rich! Being a gambling type, Mel decided he would take the chance. Besides, even at twelve years old, Mel thought that most people he knew were somewhat crazy, so the idea of being rich and a little crazy did not bother him much.

Just after Mel and his father had finished doing the supper dishes, the phone rang. Mel ran to answer the phone. Picking it up, he answered, "Dread residence, Mel speaking." The voice on the other end was crying. It was little Bonnie.

"Bonnie, what's wrong?"

It's my grandmother. She is in Mercy Hospital. She had a bad fall and broke her hip."

"Is she going to be all right?" Mel asked.

"After Grandma has her surgery, they will keep her here for a few days and then m ybe temporarily in a convalescent home somewhere here in Ainsworth. Mel," Bonnie asked, "do you think I could spend a few nights at your house? I don't want to be alone in my grandmother's big old house. Besides, we could talk and spend some time together."

"You know you can always stay here. Hang on and I will get the 'big okay' from my dad."

Walking into the kitchen, Mel quickly informed his dad about little Bonnie's grandma. Then he asked if little Bonnie could spent a few days with them.

"Of course she can stay here. That's not a problem," Mel's dad said, winking at Mel. "She's just like part of the family and can stay as long as she needs to."

"My dad says you can stay as long as you need to."

"Oh, that is so good to know," Bonnie answered with a sigh of great relief.

"Where are you calling from, Bonnie?"

"I am at Mercy General Hospital,calling from the front desk phone." "Listen, partner, my dad and I will be there very shortly to pick you up."Then Mel, with as much confidence as he could muster, added, "Your grandmother is in good hands. She has a strong will and is getting great medical care, and she has the love of God on her side. We will be there to pick you up soon. I cannot wait to see you, little Bonnie. I sure have missed you. I just don't know what a private eye investigator like myself is to do without his assistant around to help solve all those mysteries in the world that are waiting for us." Mel laughed happily.

CHAPTER 8

Grandmother's Busy or It's a Great Day for a Road Trip

Bonnie was waiting in front of Mercy General Hospital when Mel and his father pulled up. Mel jumped out and opened the car door for Bonnie.

Mel and his father greeted Bonnie as she got into their car. "Hello," she said. "I so appreciate you picking me up and letting me stay at your house for a few days, Pastor Dread."

"Like I said earlier to Mel, you are part of our family. You can stay forever if you need to, so not to worry. Just know that your grandmother is in God's hands and we h ve each other. With the Lord's help, I pray everything will turn out just as God intends it to."

Mel chimed in, "My dad's right, Bonnie. Some things are just meant to be."

Soon they were sitting at the kitchen table. Mel warmed Bonnie up some leftover spaghetti in the microwave. Setting the plate down in front of her, he said, "Well, Bonnie, my dad wants to take us to Des Moines, Iowa this week to show us the cathedral I have told you so much about. You know, Bonnie, the one my great-grandfather helped work on? He has to go there for an overnight church-related business meeting and thought he would drag us along."

Bonnie had been busy slurping on her spaghetti, as she thought half of the fun of eating spaghetti was playing with the long, stringy pasta. With big eyes popped out, spaghetti hanging from her mouth, and tomato sauce dripping from her chin, she slurped up the tangling pasta. Then she wiped the tomato sauce from her face, looked at Pastor Dread who was sitting at the kitchen table drinking some hot tea, and said, "Gee, it's always fun to do a road trip. How long does it take to get to… where did you say? Des Moines, Iowa?"

Little Bonnie winked at Mel as she continued to pretend she had never been to Iowa.

"We can leave early on Tuesday morning, and it takes roughly seven hours by car. We will return late Wednesday night or maybe stay until Thursday. So pack light, kids. Remember, this is a business trip."

Both Mel and Bonnie looked at Mel's father. Mel said, "little Bonnie and I will be no problem at all, Dad. You handle your business, and we will be happy to be somewhere—"Mel stopped to reconsider what he was about to say, "Somewhere where there is a lot of Dread family history to learn about."

"Son, how would you and Bonnie like to visit your great-grandparents' gravesite? They're buried in a cemetery very close to the Des Moines Cathedral."

"Wow, Dad," Mel exclaimed, "that would be terrific, as long as Bonnie wouldn't mind visiting Dread people." He looked at Bonnie. "Bonnie, you will sleep in the spare guest room just down the hall. Mel can show you where the room is and give you towels and anything else you need. He is the man who knows where everything is in this house. Tomorrow you two can pack what you will need for our trip, and before we know it we will be on the road heading on a short summer vacation. I only wish it were to Disneyland in California. Someday, Mel, when we can afford it, we will take some long-deserved vacations, I promise."

His dad walked away into his study and picked up his Bible, sat in his favorite easy chair, and read until 10:00 PM, just like on most every night Mel could remember.

Tuesday morning, as most days do, showed up right when it was supposed to. It was still dark out when their car pulled out of the driveway and headed down the road. Mel and Bonnie spent the next few hours sleeping in the backseat. It was not hard for them to fall asleep as they had stayed up very late the night before engaged in investigative conversation.

At about nine in the morning, the car stopped. Mel, waking little Bonnie, pointed his finger at a sign for restrooms. Mel's dad, having just returned from using the toilet, said to the two of them, "It's a rest stop. You two go use the restrooms and don't forget to wash both hands. Then how about we get some cold drinks and snacks from the candy and soda machines over there and get back on the road as time is a-wasting."

As the kids snacked on junk food, the highway slipped past. Soon a sign on the side of the highway indicated they were fifty miles from Des Moines.

"We will be there very soon now," said Mr. Dread. "I have reserved us rooms at the Manor Inn on Grand Avenue, where I have stayed many times in the past. It is clean and serves a great continental breakfast. Just down the street is a diner that serves the best hamburgers and fries you have ever tasted. To top it off, they have milkshakes that are out of this world. The food there is so good, you might think it is a sin." Pastor Dread chuckled.

Of course, they were all hungry for some real food, being tired of the junk food from the rest stop they had been consuming for the last four hours of the trip across Nebraska and Iowa. It was the same route that Bonnie and Mel had taken just about two weeks ago. They both wondered, pulling into the parking lot of the Manor Inn on Grand Avenue, whether one of them would slip up and tip off Mel's dad to the fact that this was not their first visit to Des Moines.

Mel's dad was right. The food at the diner was deliriously delicious. They all ordered large combinations of hamburgers, vinegar fries, and double churned milkshakes.

Mel's dad ha an appointment at 2:00 p.m. with one of the church officials at the cathedral. Bonnie and Mel decided that they would hang out and wait for Mel's father to finish his meeting, and then the three of them would explore the church where Mel's great-grandfather had been a young mason and artisan.

Walking up the steps of the cathedral, both Mel and little Bonnie were both thinking the same unthinkable thing: what if they ran into Mary Ann Leslie Claire, or anyone else who might recognize them? They had no choice but to try to keep their secrets to themselves and hope for the best. Soon

Pastor Dread disappeared through a door that read, "Office of Mary Ann Leslie Claire, Internal Affairs."

"Holy mackerel," Mel said to Bonnie. "My dad is here to see Mary Ann Leslie Claire."

Taking Bonnie's hand, he pulled her quietly over to a door and pulled on the handle. It opened, and they both ducked inside and closed the door. They walked down a hallway and saw a second door. They once again scurried through the door. As fast as they could, they closed it behind them.

They were standing at the entrance to the main pulpit in the enormous room where thousands came to worship throughout the years. It was as silent as if sound had not yet been discovered. It was a scary place, Bonnie thought. She grabbed Mel's hand. Mel took her hand, leading her back over to the statue that he thought had been made by Mel Porter Dread I.

Mel stood there in front of the statue. It seemed as if it were glowing. Letting go of Bonnie's hand, Mel reached into his pocket and took out his Swiss Army knife. Mel got down on his belly and slithered and squeezed until he was behind the statue. Bonnie just stood there with her eyes roaming around the giant room. She could feel her knees start to shake. She did not like any situations that could possibly make her pee her pants.

Squatting down by Mel's legs, which were sticking out from behind the statue, she asked in a low voice, "What in God's name are you doing back there, Mel P. Dread?"

Mel had been digging a hole in the back of statue with his jackknife. He had managd to dig through the outer layer of the hundred-year-old painted fresco statue. Mel was now digging into the plaster layer, which was about four inches thick. As Mel continued to dig, little Bonnie sat curled up at the base of the statue, holding on to Mel's legs.

The big room, which had been only moments ago been aglow from the sun setting through the huge stained glass windows, was now dark except for candles burning in all the vestibules and niches throughout the cathedral. Five small red exit signs could be seen far away in the darkness. They could lead little Bonnie to safety if she should decide to get up and run, which she felt inspired to do. Suddenly a door on the other side of the cathedral opened, causing Bonnie to almost pee her pants. She saw a man and a woman standing in the doorway, and a voice that sounded very much like Mary Ann Leslie Claire's rang through the empty cathedral. "Hello,

hello, hello!" Little Bonnie's heart beat a mile a minute as she began pulling on Mel's legs, trying to drag him out from behind the bigger-than-life statue of Jesus. Mel tried to gather his wits together. Mel said, "Hello."

Mel's dad answered, "Mel! Mel! What are you doing, son? You two were supposed to meet me after my meeting! It ended a few hours ago."

Mel took Bonnie's hand and walked over to where his father was standing, saying, "I am sorry, Dad. We fell asleep on the floor in front of the statue of Jesus over there in the grotto. I am pretty sure it was a statue that was made by Mel P. Dread, my great-grandfather."

Mel's dad asked, "Mel, why is it so very important for you to know what your grandfather actually laid his hands on? Can you not just appreciate that he was a part of this entire historical cathedral? Your grandfather was a devoted religious man, and he always gave all he had to the church he loved more than anything except his devoted wife, Bonnie."

Bonnie breaking the silence, said, "Bonnie—why, what a lovely name. I am positively sure she was a lady as lovely as was her name." Little Bonnie was smiling from ear to ear so as not to show anyone what was actually going on inside her head. Her mind was exploding with fear and concern.

Mel once again reiterated, "I am terribly sorry, Dad. You have not introduced us to this lovely lady standing beside you." Slick as baby oil on a baby's butt, Mel was making his move to elevate the tension that still lingered heavily in the air of the church.

"Dad, Bonnie and I are starving. Did you not promise to take us out for some pizza?"

Taking Mary Ann Leslie Claire's hand, Mel said, "My name's Mel. This is my friend, Bonnie." He squeezed the lady's hand so hard she could not help but say, "Ouch. My name's Mary Ann Leslie Claire. It's nice to meet you all."

We would love for you, ma'am," Mel said, "to join us for some pizza this evening, although we shall most certainly understand if you have other obligations. Maybe we could come by tomorrow and you could give us a more formal tour of your beautiful cathedral?"

Mary Ann Leslie Claire did not quite know what to make of these two youngsters who had stayed at the shelter only weeks earlier. They were up to something, but she did not have a clue of what it was, so she thought it wise to play along for now.

"I am dreadfully sorry. I do have prior commitments. It was my privilege to meet you, Bonnie and Mel. I will look forward to seeing you two tomorrow. Pastor Dread, why don't you and these two dear, sweet children join me here at the mission shelter for a nutritious hot meal? We open the gate at six a.m. Can I plan to see you for breakfast?"

Mel's dad said, "We would love to see you for breakfast, Ms. Claire. See you in the morning." Locking the door of the cathedral, they all said good night and went their separate ways.

Mel said, "Dad, would it be all right if we ordered pizza from our hotel room?"

"You're reading my mind, Son. Let's pig out on pizza. Maybe they have a 'Pig out Pizza' here in Des Moines," his dad said, trying to make his best oink noise.

Bonnie laughed, and Mel said, "Last one back to the room has to do the dishes." They all laughed, but they just strolled down Grand Avenue toward the Manor Inn, which was just up the street on the left.

Mel's dad ordered a pizza while Bonnie and Mel took turns using the shower and got into their pajamas. There was a knock at their door, and Mel jumped up to open it, expecting see a pizza delivery guy. Instead it was a motel attendant with a fold-up bed. "You called for a bed?" the guy at the door asked.

"Yes," Mel's dad yelled from the bathroom. "Would you set the bed up, please?"

The young motel attendant rolled the bed in and unlocked its sides, and Mel helped him unfold the bed.

"Hello." There was another voice outside the room. Bonnie yelled, "The pizza's here."

Mel yelled, "Dad, the pizza's here."

The motel attendant left the room, saying, "Good night."

Mel was quick to introduce himself to the pretty girl, who was holding a large pizza box, "Hello. My name's Mel P. Dread, Detective Mel P. Dread. How much do we owe you for the pizza and the soda?"

The tall, blond-haired girl pulled the receipt out of her pocket smiling, and, said, "Hello. That will be $25.78. Would you like some hot crushed peppers, Detective?"

Bonnie said, "Yes, please, some hot peppers." Then she motioned for Mel to go get the pizza money from his dad, who was still in the bathroom.

They scarfed down the large pizza in record time, and it made them all sleepy. They decided that Mel would sleep on the rollaway bed, little Bonnie in the one single bed, and Pastor Dread in the other. It seemed they had just gone to sleep when the phone rang. It was the front desk calling to wake the three of them up. They all had another big day ahead of them, and Mel was first to hit the showers.

It was a cool morning as they walked down Grand Avenue toward the mission shelter. They arrived at 7:15. Ms. Claire w s already there.

She was talking to a couple of guys, who were busy eating their breakfast. She motioned the three of them to get in line and pick up a tray. She pretended to put food on her imaginary tray, miming perfectly from across the dining hall. The three got in the breakfast line, and soon they were at a table sitting down to enjoy their meal.

Ms. Mary Ann Leslie Claire, with a hot cup of tea, sat down next Pastor Dread across the table from the two little people with their mouths full of scrambled eggs. She smiled at little Bonnie and Mel sitting there, and she gave each of them a grimacing wink of her eye. Pastor Dread cocked his head, looked at Mel, and said, "Slow down, you two. Where are your manners?"

"Sorry, Dad," Mel tried to say, still with scrambled eggs hindering his ability to speak clearly.

Bonnie was so nervous she continued eating her breakfast. She knew at any moment Mel's dad would learn about their having already met Ms. Mary Ann Leslie Claire and about their previous trip to Des Moines. There were so many cats to let out of the bag, she thought. Once so many cats get out of a bag, you can never, no matter how hard you try, get them all back in.

The pastor was busy talking, not having a clue about any of the cats being about to be let out of a bag. He was here on church business, asking questions about the church's finances and the food and shelter program that was to be closing its doors soon.

"Is there any way to save the homeless mission and shelter?" he asked her.

"No, I am afraid not. Only some kind of miracle could let us continue to love and provide for the poor as God would have us do." Pastor Dread took that opportunity to add, "God loves the poor as much as he does those who he has blessed with gold and silver. I believe that with all my heart and soul."

"Amen," Mary Ann Leslie Claire exclaimed. "Amen," Mel repeated.

Bonnie just nodded. She was determined to keep her mouth shut for fear it would be her mouth that let all those cats out of the bag. She was determined just this once to be seen, not heard.

Pastor Dread excused himself and headed for a bathroom. No sooner had he gotten out of ear range, than Mel said, "My dear Mary Ann Leslie Claire, you must have a thousand questions," to which she replied, "I do."

Bonnie, finally opening her mouth to speak, said, "The only reason we were here the first time was that we were searching for lost treasure— gold coins, enough treasure to make us the richest two kids in the whole world."

Bonnie was right. Once she opened her mouth, the cats were getting out of the bag two at a time. Mel did not even try to stop little Bonnie. Mel knew the gig was up soon and wanted to be sure to take care of any detective work while he was still in Des Moines with his dad, little Bonnie, his faithful assistant, and their new friend, the head of the mission itself, Ms. Mary Ann Leslie Claire. Mel knew it was time to let a few of those cats out of hiding. It was time to show a big part of his hand, time to find out for once and for all where the one ton of lost gold coins had disappeared over one hundred years ago.

He was interrupted by his father saying, "Do either of you two kids need to use the restrooms?"

Bonnie abruptly quit talking. Mel said, "Yes, Bonnie, we should go use the restrooms." They stood up and walked quickly around the corner, out of sight from Pastor Dread and Ms. Claire. "I am so sorry, Mel. I couldn't help myself, and I just felt we had to give the dear lady an explanation. Did I let all the cats out of the bag, Melvin P. Dread?"

"No," he said, reaching in his pocket and pulling out a gold coin. "Oh my Gawd, Mel," Bonnie said, grabbing the gold coin out of his hand. "Where did this coin come from?"

Mel looked at her and smiled. "I dug it out of the back of Christ's statue."

"What? Why did you not show me before now?"

"Because," Mel answered, "in order to solve any good mystery, one does need to be careful to let things fall into place." Taking the gold coin out of

Bonnie's hand and putting back in his pocket, he said, "You'd better pee" and walked into the men's restroom.

Little Bonnie and Mel returned, and they both knew they had some splainin' to do to Pastor Dread; he looked a tiny bit agitated. In his not-so-great Ricky Ricardo voice, Mel sat down, looked at his dad, and said, "I got some splainin' to do, Dad!"

"What's this I hear from Ms. Mary Ann Leslie Claire that you two are here looking for the Dread family treasure? Did I not tell you how ridiculous those old fabricated stories are? I beg of you to listen to me. Come to your senses, please, Son," his dad pleaded emotionally.

Mel, without saying a word, stood up, reached in his pocket, and pulled out his clenched fist. He held it out in front of his dad and said, "I mean no disrespect, dear father, but I must disagree with you," opening his hand and revealing a shiny gold coin.

CHAPTER 9

A Streak of Luck or What Are You Digging For?

L ittle Bonnie looked at Mel's father and said, "Yes, Pastor Dread. I also must disagree with you. That's only one coin. We know where there are lots more! Mel said there are a lot more where that one came from."

Mel's dad, who was still examining the gold coin, said, "Good gracious. God almighty, Mel. Who would have thought?"

Mary Ann Leslie Claire just stood there repeating, "Oh my, oh my, oh my!" Finally she said, "I cannot wait to hear where you found this coin, let alone where there might be more."

Pastor Dread chimed in, "Yes, Mel, can you show us where this gold coin is?"

"Not a problem, Dad," Mel said, motioning them to follow him. "You just follow me." They got up and did just what Mel had asked them to do. Little Bonnie walked at Mel's side as they headed for the cathedral, followed closely by Mary Ann Leslie Claire with Pastor Dread right behind them all.

Mel led them all into the empty cathedral. They walked over to the statue of Jesus Christ holding a golden cross, with Jesus's head tilted up and eyes looking divinely heavenward. Mel reached into his pocket and took out his jackknife. He got down on the floor and crawled once again back behind the beautiful, handpainted sculpture of Jesus.

Bonnie said to them both, "Not to worry," taking hold of Mary Ann Leslie Claire's hand with her left hand and then taking Pastor Dread's right hand in her other. Little Bonnie proudly announced that Mel P. Dread was simply the best when it came to finding lost treasure.

The two adults were fixated on Mel, who had been using his jackknife to retrieve another gold coin. After a few short minutes, Mel backed out from behind the statue. Standing up, he opened his hand and revealed two more gold coins. Bonnie was smiling ear to ear. She was so proud of Mel that she could hardly contain herself. She leaned over and kissed Mel on the cheek. No one noticed but Mel.

Mel's father and Mary Ann Leslie Claire stood there in shock, completely awed by the thought that they were possibly standing in front of a statue containing one ton of gold coins minted in 1855.

Mel did not know what any of this meant. He was thinking that because the gold coins were hidden in the cathedral, they all belonged not to the Dread family but rather the church. He figured that the money would be used to help all those who depended on the church. Now the church would be able to use the gold coins to continuing offering food and shelter for all the needy people.

Soon it was time for the three of them to say good-bye and begin their seven-hour drive back to their own beds once again. Mel and Bonnie took up the back seats, where they giggled and whispered back and forth, which would hopefully make the trip pass more quickly. Mel would be glad to be back in Ainsworth. He knew something now that no one else yet knew. A few cats were still hiding in the bag, and Mel definitely planned to keep them there until he decided differently. But first he neede to get a good night's rest in his own bed. For Mel P. Dread, tomorrow was a brand new day. It would be a wonderful day to look for some more of the Dread family treasure.

After the seven hour drive, they were finally home. They had unloaded the bags from the car and had managed to get them into the house. Bonnie would spend yet another night at Mel's house, as her grandmother was still in the hospital. It had only been a few days since she had fallen and broke her hip. The hospital said she was doing well but was sleeping most of the time. Bonnie was relieved to think that her grandmother would be back on her feet before too long, back to being her pleasant and wonderful self.

Not much was said. They were all tired, and even Bonnie knew the routine. After they took turns using the bathroom and brushing their teeth, they each went to their bedrooms and crawled into bed for the rest they all needed to get.

*   *   *

It was Thursday. Mel was outside on the front porch swinging back and forth on the old wooden bench swing. The old swing hung by chains from the porch ceiling. Bonnie sat down next to him on the swing. The swing did not stop swinging. She got on with perfect timing. Neither of them spoke. They sat there for the next twenty minutes, both of them staring across the street.

Finally Bonnie said, "I guess this means we're not going to be the richest twelve-year-olds in the world after all, huh, Mel?" Mel just sat there, swinging back and forth.

"Mel," little Bonnie went on, "you should be so very proud of yourself. You not only solved a hundred-year-old mystery but found where your great-grandfather hid all that gold. The gold coins will be such a blessing to the church. Because of you, Detective Mel P. Dread, the Des Moines Cathedral will have more than enough money to help feed and clothe the hungry and the homeless."

Mel finally looked at Bonnie and smiled. "You helped me, Bonnie. I could not have imagined finding the gold coins without you. You're the best!"

Bonnie could tell Mel was most definitely still up to something. "Mel," she said, "I know you're still up to something. What are you planning to do now?"

Mel replied, "Go to church."

"Go to church? What do you mean, Mel, go to church? What church?"

"My dad's church. The church that both my grandfather and great-grandfather built," he answered. "There are still some stories and folklore that tell about my great-grandfather having divided the gold coins up and hidden a part of the treasure somewhere else. I suspect some of the artwork in our church here in Ainsworth was brought here from the Des Moines Cathedral."

Getting off the swing, Mel stood up and stretched, saying, "Let's go get some breakfast. Then, Bonnie, after we eat, Melvin P. Dread, private detective, needs your assistance once again."

"What are you still looking for, Mel, if I can ask?"

Mel answered, "I still need to get a few more stray cats out of the bag!"

Following Mel into the house, little Bonnie said, "Well, Mel, you know my number one talent just happens to be…" She giggled and made a drum sound. "Letting cats out of the bags."

They both laughed and headed for the kitchen to find something to eat for breakfast. In the kitchen sat Mel's dad, watching the small TV that sat on the counter next to the coffeepot. The toaster and the can opener sat beside a big yellow cat that looked quite real at first glance. But it was just a big ceramic cookie jar.

"Mel, come here," his dad hollered, just as Mel and little Bonnie entered the room. He said, "You won't believe what's on the TV!"

There, on the screen, was the morning news doing an investigative report on the Des Moines Cathedral. They were interviewing Mary Ann Leslie Claire. All three of them stood there watching the TV, speechless. They intently listened as she was being interviewed. It was good to hear her answering all of the questions the three of them had been wondering about regarding the cathedral's intentions for the substantial amount of money the church had suddenly had in its possession.

Ending the interview, the reporter asked if there was any last thing she would like to say. Mary Ann Leslie Claire looked directly into the camera and said, "God can certainly work in mysterious ways. It was only through the grace of God almighty himself that after more than one hundred years we have been graced by two magnificent young children who were responsible for finding the lost gold coins. The two young, lovely children were the ones who actually led us, the church officials, to where the fortune of lost gold coins had been hidden."

"Will there be a reward for these two young people?" the interviewer asked.

Smiling into the camera, she said, "The church believes all those good deeds we do here on earth will be repaid by the Lord when we get to heaven. So the church opens its arms to accept this bountiful blessing which has come our way. It will be used in ways that the church feels God would have it be used for: to help the countless upon countless of others who need the mission shelter's continual help and support."

"Now let's go back to you in the CBX studio, with your host of the morning show, Mat O'Donnell." As the cameraman faded back, he ended with a shot of the magnificent cathedral in the background. The TV morning news anchorman said, "What a wonderful story. Thanks for that, Tim Casselberry, one of CBX's roving reporters. We all know God will surely bless those two kids from Nebraska. God bless those amazing twelve-year-olds who found the well hidden treasure. By the way, you might be wondering what all the gold is estimated to be worth. The gold coins are valued at well over…" Chuckling, Mat told his audience it was so much money he did not know how to read the number.

"Trust me," Mat O'Donnell said into the TV camera, "it's priceless." Then he added, "I sure wish I had just one of those priceless coins in my pocket! Now let us scoot over to the weather board with the weather lady herself, Wendy Winters."

Reaching over and turning off the TV set, Pastor Dread said, "Well, that was nice. You two should be very proud of yourselves." "I am glad we could all be here to watch it together," Mel said, looking at little Bonnie.

"Yes," said little Bonnie. "Now we know we are still poor." She rolled her eyes up in her head in dismay.

Mel got out two bowls and a big variety pack of cereal. Bonnie got out the milk and stuck two pieces of white toast into the toaster. Mel pushed down the knob as he pulled open the drawer to get out a couple of spoons. Mel said, "There are bananas over there that need to be eaten."

His father w s once again busy reading the morning paper.

He did not say another word.

Mel sliced bananas on top of a bowl of puffed wheat and a bowl of puffed rice and poured milk over the cereal. Then he and Bonnie each took a bowl and began to eat, both trying to comprehend that well known concept that says one should always get a fair wage for a hard day of work.

CHAPTER 10

Be Careful, Someone Could Get Hurt or Take Two Pills and Call Me in the Morning

Bonnie thought, *NO soup for us! It's funny. I have not heard anyone say in such a long time, it seems, the phrase, "God loves the poor as much as he loves the more fortunate."* She knew somewhere in this story was a lesson from God. At least her grandmother would always tell her, "Little Bonnie Lou Starr, trust that God has a plan for you, sweetie!" Well, God's plan for Bonnie was certainly not the same plan she had had, which was to be the one of the richest twelve-year-olds in the world by now.

Little Bonnie looked upward as if God might be up there looking down at her. Mel said, "Bonnie, are you all right?"

"Yes," she said. "I was thinking out loud to myself again." Mel said, "See you later, Dad."

Bonnie said, "Good-bye Pastor Dread."

"Later," Pastor Dread said, but he did not look up from the morning newspaper.

Soon they were out on the front porch, unlocking their bikes and heading off to the church. It was not even Sunday, they both thought as they mounted their bikes and rode north toward the Ainsworth church where, with any luck, Mel hoped to find a few more of those lost gold coins his great-grandfather had hidden. Bonnie did not have a clue what Mel was once again up to, but she would trust that he knew.

As they rode down the street, little Bonnie said to Mel, "Mel, school starts pretty soon."

Mel replied, "I know. I have been trying my darnedest not to think about us going back to school." They pulled their bikes around to the back of the empty church and hid them in some tall grass. Quickly they headed over to the church to see how hard it would be to break into.

Mel had been going to this church for as long as he could remember. It was the only regular church he had attended. It was funny, he thought, how he was able see his life's past moments in his mind. He could still recall everything that had happened to him, even as a baby. Few people have the ability to recall every day of their lives. Mel was one of those people. He had no idea yet how useful this gift of memory would turn out to be later in his life.

Mel stood staring at the church. "Mel, are you just going to stand there, or are we here for some particular reason?" Bonnie suddenly interrupted Mel's thoughts. "Mel Porter Dread, are you listening to me?"

Hearing Bonnie's voice, Mel was suddenly brought back into the real world. "Sorry," Mel said. "I was just catching my breath."

Bonnie said, "Well I'd help you catch it, except I'm still trying to catch mine. Where to, Sherlock?"

Mel went around to the side of the church, where steps led down to the basement of the church. It was easy to see the door at the bottom of the stairs in the bright day ight. Mel was leading the way, and Bonnie was close behind him. At the bottom of the stairs was a metal door with a big lock right b low the brass doorknob.

Bonnie grabbed the door handle and turned it. "The door is locked," she said, as she tried to push the door cpen. "Okay, Mel P. Dread, I bet you one of those six gold coins that not even you are going to get in this church building by using this door to get there!"

Mel said, "Okay, it's a bet. I never guessed you to be a betting kind of gal—er, girlfriend—er, I mean, assistant."

Both children blushed. Mel reached into his pocket and took out a bunch of keys. Picking out one old brass key, Mel stuck it into the lock, gave it a turn, and it opened the lock. "Any other bets you would like to make, my dear assistant?" Mel giggled.

"Ha, ha, ha... very funny, Mr. Smarty pants Mel. You make Houdini's tricks seem, how should I put it, much more impressive then I had originally thought."

Pulling Bonnie into the dark room, Mel locked the door behind them.

"Mel," Bonnie said, "I cannot see a thing. Are there any lights down here?" She hung on to Mel's shirt tails as Mel, with both hands stretched out in front of him, moved through the big, dark basement, trying to find a light he could turn on.

"Well, just great," Bonnie said. "Where is your flashlight, Detective Dread?"

Mel said, "Uh oh. It's in my backpack, out with our bikes, Bonnie. Stay right here, Bonnie. Don't move! I will be right back with my flashlight. It will only take a minute."

As Bonnie sat waiting by herself in the dark basement of the church, she started to think about what a summer this had been for her and her best friend. Sitting there in the dark, she thought about the first day she saw Mel from her grandmother's porch. He was getting the mail out of his mailbox across the street. Little Bonnie felt a curious attraction to this stranger immediately. She was so infatuated with Mel that she followed him for three days before she found him trapped at the bottom of that well. It certainly was a place that Mel could not ignore her. She was thankful to have saved his life, as she knew meeting Mel had definitely changed her life.

Suddenly there was an awful crash. Bonnie yelled, "Are you all right, Mel?" but there was no answer. "Oh my goodness," Bonnie said. "Mel, Mel!"

But he still did not answer her. The blackness was filled with only silence. Scrambling to her feet, Bonnie, moving as quickly as she could in the pitch-dark basement, began to feel her way over in the direction he thought the awful noise had come from. Finally Bonnie made her way over to the back of the basement, where she could feel lots of big books all over the floor. There were hundreds of heavy books, and she could feel a big wooden bookcase in among them. It had toppled over and had obviously killed her best friend, Mel.

"Oh my God," little Bonnie wailed loudly. "Oh dear God, not my Mel." She tried to locate Mel's body under the mound of old church books.

First Bonnie found a leg, and then she found Mel's other leg. She worked at clearing away all the books in the pitchblack room. Little Bonnie was crying. She laid her head on Mel's chest and whispered, "I will always love you, Mel P. Dread."

"Well, I will always love you too, Bonnie," Mel replied as he rubbed his head.

Mel asked Bonnie, "Where in tarnation are we?"

"Oh my Gawd, Mel, you've lost your mind!" little Bonnie screamed.

Mel answered, "It's not my mind I've hurt. It's my arm. I think I broke my arm."

Little Bonnie said as if she felt Mel's pain, "I am so sorry! Mel, just tell me how I can assist you." In the dark she could not see Mel's tears rolling down his boyish face. He was crying from the pain of his newly broken right arm. The pain was intense. His arm and head really hurt him, but he knew he must remain calm and try his best not to panic.

"Bonnie, I am afraid the basement door is blocked by this huge wooden bookcase. So if we are to get out of here, we will have to find another way. Bonnie, there is a staircase that leads up to the inside of the church. At the top of those steps, you will find a single light switch, which should turn on some lights down here," Mel told her.

Bonnie answered, "Not a problem, Detective Dread. I am at your disposal." Trying to make Mel as comfortable as she could, she helped him to sit up and cradle his right arm with his left. Bonnie, without any hesitation, knew that Mel was counting on her to save the day.

Pretending to be on a TV show, Bonnie made believe she was competing for millions of dollars of gold coins. Bravely, little Bonnie began making her way through the dark obstacle course. In the pitch dark, she would attempt to break the all-time world record for maneuvering through booby traps, cobwebs, and driedout old mouse and rat poop—not to mention any icky spiders that might reside in the building—in her search for the lights. Bonnie hated spiders, but that would not stop her from getting beyond the dirt, the debris, and the endless possible dead ends. Nothing would stop her as she struggled toward her objective of turning on some lights.

She managed to get across the church basement unscathed.

Little Bonnie could feel herself nearing victory as she stubbed her foot on the bottom of the stairs that would lead to the light switch. Bounding up the steps, Bonnie felt that victory was very close at hand. Without missing a step, little Bonnie yelled, "I have found the light switch!"

Reaching up, she flicked the light switch to the "on" position. At the same time, she lost her balance and tumbled to the bottom of the steps. Little Bonnie landed on the cold basement floor with a thud. Mel heard the hideous sound echo loudly throughout the dark basement.

Mel yelled, "Are you all right, Bonnie Lou Starr?"

"Oh my gracious," little Bonnie said, sitting up and taking a moment to gain her composure. After a moment, Bonnie yelled back to Mel, "The good news is that I have accomplished my mission."

Mel could see that Bonnie had managed to turn on a few lights here and there throughout the darkness.

Bonnie made her way back across the gigantic church basement. She saw Mel still sitting where she had left him. Holding out her left arm and supporting it with her right, she then said, "The bad news is, Mel P. Dread, I too seem to have broken my arm."

"Well, when the going gets tough, the tough get going, they say," Mel replied. "At least we will still be able to hold hands. We're quite the team!"

"Mel," she asked, "Will you sign my cast if we get out of here alive?" Tears began running down little Bonnie's face.

Mel, getting to his feet, replied, "Only if you will sign mine." Finding some old white sheets that were covering some of the church's Christm s decorations, Mel made them each a sling for their now-useless arms. Mel said, "We should try to get out of here, and then I think we should go see your grandmother in the hospital. While we're there, maybe we should have our arms looked at."

Bonnie nodded her head in agreement with Mel.

Unfortunately, they soon found out that the only other way out of the church basement was locked, and there was no key to open the big door.

Bonnie looked at Mel and said, "Okay, Mr. Mel P. Houdini. Let's see you get us out of this chained and locked box."

Cradling his broken arm, Mel was snooping around. Bonnie sat down on a cardboard box under one of the few hanging sixty-watt bulbs that dispersed light throughout the entire large church basement. Mel had not been gone long when he returned with some bottled water and a first-aid kit. Mel handed Bonnie two pain pills and a bottle of water, and then he took two of the pills for himself.

Bonnie watched as Mel collected blankets and pillows for them to lie down on. He had even managed to find something to eat from the church's disaster supply storage cupboards. Bonnie, in a low, raspy voice, asked, "How long will we have to stay down here, Mel?"

Mel looked at his watch. It was 8:35 p.m., which meant it was already dark outside. They had spent the last five hours trapped in the church basement, managing only to break their arms. Thinking, Mel said, "Tomorrow at nine a.m., my father will probably come here to prepare for his weekend services. He must also have the church opened for the church organist to practice with the choir. So unless something changes, we are stuck down here for at least the night."

Mel smiled at little Bonnie as she cradled her broken left arm with her right and said to her, "I hope you enjoy your stay. Shall I fix us some supper, my dear assistant?"

They ate some dried beef jerky, along with a bland, awful-tasting nutritional bar, washing them down with the bottled water Mel had found. Soon, they both started feeling the effects of the pain pills they had taken.

"Oh, wow," Bonnie said in a woozy voice. "Those pills you gave me are making me drowsy."

Mel, who was sounding quite woozy as well, said, "Oh wow, me too. We should lie down and get comfortable." He handed Bonnie another pill, saying, "Take it. You'll sleep much better."

Mel took another pill as well, and then he said drowsily, "Not to have any worries, Bonnie Lou Starr. With me here by your side, you don't have to be afraid. I promise…"

The two of them quickly fell asleep. Unfortunately, the pain pills did not stop their arms from feeling broken. They just allowed them to fall asleep for their long night in the old church basement.

Meanwhile, Mel's dad had fallen asleep on the couch in the living room. When he got up in the middle of the night and headed to his bedroom, he had no idea that Mel and little Bonnie were not upstairs in their own beds, fast asleep. He could not know they were trapped in the basement of the church the Dread family had built a long, long time ago.

Mel and Bonnie spent the long night lying on the floor, hoping that any minute they would hear sounds coming from upstairs in the church. Drifting in and out of consciousness, Bonnie could hear the sound of an organ playing. Mel heard it too! Mel slowly stood up. Once on both his feet, he reached down and helped Bonnie get to her feet as well.

Mel said, "Here we go again, Lucy. We got some more splainin' to do!" Standing at the top of the stairs leading into the church, Mel and Bonnie started pounding on the door with their good fists, yelling, "Hello, hello, can anybody hear us?"

They stopped yelling and listened. They could not hear the organist playing or the choir singing. Leaning against the big wood door they both listened, hoping to hear someone upstairs in the church. The door suddenly opened, and looking at them was none other than Mel's father. Behind Pastor Dread stood the church organist and about twenty or so choir singers, all staring at Mel and little Bonnie. Mel and Bonnie stood there looking as if they had been through some horrible ordeal to say the least.

"Oh,my son,what on earth are you doing in the church basement?" Seeing they had been injured, he aske ,"How badly are you hurt?"

Mel just said, "Morning, dad. I got some more splainin' to do. But first, I think all you need to know is that we just spent last night down here in the church basement. We got locked in down here, and as we were trying to get out we both somehow managed to break our arms."

Then Mel added "I think it is imperative you drive us to the hospital, Dad. We really should get these broken arms attended too, don't you think?"

The drive to Mercy General Hospital took no more than ten minutes. Their car was met at the emergency room entrance by two wheelchairs. They were both wheeled out of sight to have their fractured arms reset and secured with some nice plaster casts. After a few hours they were ready to get back into the family car, sporting new white plaster casts. It would be a day or two before Bonnie and Mel would feel like trying to explain to Pastor Dread the reason they had been in the church basement in the first place. Mel's dad just could not believe how his son was so set on doing things the hard way. After all, all Mel had to do was ask, and Pastor Dread would have let him investigate the church basement.

Mel reminded Pastor Dread so much of his own father. Mel's spirit was even larger than any of the Dread men's so far, it seemed to him. He looked forward to watching Mel grow into a strong young man, a man who at a respectable age would settle down and have some little Dreads of his own to carry on the family name. Maybe a few would turn out larger than life as well, Pastor Dread thought. On the way home Pastor Dread pulled into Tanya's Monster Burger and stopped in front of the menu board with a speaker attached to it. They were looking at the menu when a voice asked if they would like to order one of the thirteen different Monster Burger specials.

Mr. Dread answered, "Yes, give me three number sevens with three iced teas—and we are hungry, so make them all your large, scary size, please!"

"Will that be all?" the voice asked.

"Yes," Mr. Dread answered politely. The voice in the box was instructed them to please pull up to the second window.

Not one word was uttered until they managed to get inside the house and find a place in the living room where they could sit and eat their grotesque, oversized burgers.

Mel and Bonnie struggled to eat their dinners. The French fries were a piece of cake to eat with one hand, but the Mighty Number Seven Monster Burger was a challenge with only one working hand. Their mouths were too busy eating fries and battling with the burgers to even try to engage in any conversation about why they were in the church basement to begin with. Mel knew sooner or later he would have some splainin' to do!

But tonight, Mel and little Bonnie's biggest battle was managing to consume, single-handedly, a Number Seven from the Monster Burger menu. Mel's schoolmates called the monster burger "The Idiot Burger" because in most cases it was more cow than the average person could chew. It came with a ton of fries and, of course, a scary-sized drink of choice. Broken arms or not, Mel and Bonnie were both lost in the world of extreme, gluttonous consumption. A one-handed battle with a Number Seven Monster Burger was enough to concentrate on at the moment.

Pastor Dread exclaimed loudly, "Before we eat any more, we forgot to give thanks! Dear Heavenly Father, we thank you for these juicy, delectable hamburgers that Tanya down at Tanya's Monster Burger has prepared for our supper. Amen."

"Amen," said Mel, and bringing up the rear, little Bonnie said, "Amen." Then they were all back at their one-handed Monster Burger challenges.

One hour later, they were feeling like idiots for trying to eat Number Seven Monster Burgers that had been supersized to the super-scary size. They now were too full and too tired, and they all just sat quietly in the living room. Then, one by one, they headed off to get some sleep.

*   *   *

It once again was Sunday morning. For the second week in a row, Mel would be staying home from church to mend his broken arm. His assistant, Bonnie, would also not be in church this Sunday morning.

Hearing his father's car pulling out of the driveway, Mel got up and found little Bonnie down in the living room eating a bowl of cornflakes.

"Morning, Detective Porter."

"Morning. How'd you sleep, Bonnie?" asked Mel.

Bonnie laughed. "The same way you did, with my arm in this plaster cast."

They both laughed as Mel headed to the kitchen to get himself a bowl of cereal.

Joining Bonnie back on the living room couch, Mel said, "There is so much splainin' to do, Bonnie!"

Bonnie said, "Sometimes my stepdad says a picture is worth a couple of hours of me trying to explain something to him." Little Bonnie, showing a bit of arrogance, said, "As the saying goes, Mel, show me the money!"

"Stepdad," Mel said, looking at little Bonnie. "You never told me your dad was a stepdad."

"Yes. It's a rather boring story, and I seldom mention it because I have always thought of him as my friend as well as a great father to me. I am blessed as we are all blessed. Sometimes it just takes the right circumstance to be able to see it. I think it is rather like hunting for lost treasure. It's the hunt that the stuff of one's life is made of, I have decided." Little Bonnie continued, "You must know that too, Mel, or you would not still aspire to be a professional private eye."

Mel, finishing his cereal, looked at Little Bonnie and said, "You are one smart cookie, Miss Bonnie Lou Starr."

Bonnie said to Mel, "My mother called again this morning. I told her I was fine, that I had a broken arm, but nothing serious," She held up her white plaster cast and made a goofy face. "I did not mention to her that you had broken your arm as well, Mel. The less my parents know the better. Trust me, if they had any idea what you and I have been up to this summer, I would be grounded for life. Life! I am very sure that I would never be allowed to see you ever again! Mel, I would rather die than let that happen."

"It's okay to keep them in the dark for now, but as my grandfather always told me, truth is always better than fiction. What that means, Bonnie, is that once you let the cats out of the bag, you have no control over where they all run off to!"

"All I know, Mel, is in one week my parents will be here to take me back to La Chicken Ville in order to start school again this fall. Mel, I don't want to go." Tears began to run down little Bonnie's cheeks, rolling across the Band-Aid on her face and then hitting her big, white, plaster cast.

Mel handed her a Kleenex, singing, "Hush, little Bonnie, don't you cry. I won't let them take you, bye, bye."

The rest of the Sunday was spent lying around, watching TV, and eating. Mel's dad once again brought home several bags of food from the good church la ies. They always made sure that Pastor Dread and Melvin Dread would not go hungry. As long as Mel had been around the church, he had been taken care of. The parishioners took care of those they felt were the most deserving, mostly their own kind of people: other good, faithful Christians who were always involved in carrying out the church's mission.

Mel stared at the TV, not having a clue about what he had been watching. He was wondering what those parishioners would say when he told them he had been reading about Buddhism. *Buddhism,* he thought. *I would be the first Buddhist in our family.* Mel, with a totally blank face, started to think maybe he could be Jewish. Mel was confused. Maybe he actually could be a Christian Buddhist, or a Jewish Christian, or even possibly a Jewish atheist Buddhist. They all seemed to have compelling arguments to support them. Mel did not know what to believe; he just knew for the time being he had to believe in himself, mostly!

The phone seemed to ring all afternoon. Pastor Dread was in the study, answering the phone and making calls himself. Pastor Dread was still talking on the phone as Mel and Bonnie went upstairs to bed. Mel had no idea what all those calls were about, but Mel sensed that the winds of change were a-blowin'. Mel knew he should be prepared for what he feared would be the wrath of God himself.

Before going to sleep that Sunday night, Mel got down on his knees, holding his good hand to his broken one. He closed his eyes and began to pray. "Dear God, I am just a twelve-year-old boy. I don't have a mom, my grandparents died when I was nine years old, and yet there is so very much I am thankful for. First, I am thankful for my dad. We both know he must also question his beliefs. Please bless little Bonnie. I know you must find her as priceless as I do, Lord. God, bless Bonnie's parents. Please help heal little Bonnie's grandmother's broken hip. Also, Lord, please take care of all the homeless people all over the world, as best you can. Oh, and just one more thing, Lord. Please do not be mad at me! I am just a confused twelve-year-old boy who has been asking questions, trying to decide wh t I really believe in."

Then Mel asked God if there shouldn't be a parable telling all his people that God loves us w ether we are rich or poor, whether we are always in question or remain steadfast, not questioning anything. "God, you made me who I am as a possibility, and only if I am allowed to fly will I be all you have intended me to be. Thank you for understanding, Mel P. Dread IV, private detective. Amen."

Falling asleep, Mel could hear the old grandfather clock that stood down on the landing. Someone must have rewound it because it had not made a sound in years.

The next morning, Mel came downstairs to find Bonnie on the couch with a bowl of cereal, listening to Mel's father intently. Mel flopped down on the other end of the couch, trying to figure out what he had missed and what his father was talking to Bonnie about.

CHAPTER 11

I Was Just Hanging Around for the Last Hundred Years or Happiness Is a Couple of Good Books

"Morning," Mel said. "Am I interrupting anythin? I can certainly go take my shower and come back in a little bit if you would like."

Bonnie said, "Relax, Mel. Your dad was telling me about one of your early childhood investigations. You were in the back yard playing and were investigating what you thought was a stray cat under the back porch." Pastor Dread and Bonnie started to giggle. "That cat turned out to be a skunk!" They both began laughing again.

Mel said, "Well, it was not funny then, and it's not that funny now!"

"Well, Son, it's time to change the subject and talk about why you two were in the church basement. I certainly have a lot of unanswered questions for you two to answer. Mel, as you know,   I spent most of yesterday afternoon talking on the phone. There soon will be a lot of changes taking place around here, Mel— changes that will affect all of us very much. But for right now, that can wait. First, you must clear up my concerns of what you and Bonnie were doing down in the church basement. What have you been up to now, Melvin P. Dread IV?"

Mel began by saying, "Dad, please be patient with me. I think it would be best if we went over to the church basement and I showed you. As little Bonnie's stepdad told her, a picture is worth a thousand words!"

Looking at his watch, Mel requested that they take one half hour to eat breakfast and get ready to go over to the church. "I hope," Mel added, "that I can show you exactly why I was in that church basement, Dad. I believe it is where my grandfather and his father hid the rest of the Dread family treasure, our share of the Dread family treasure, long ago." Mel was trying his best to not sound too excited, Both little Bonnie and Mel's father stared at Mel with big eyes and mystified expressions. Mel's dad did not say a word.

Little Bonnie said, "Well, Detective Dread, what are you waiting for? Get eating your breakfast because trust us, your dad and I are ready for you to finally put all your cards on the table. We cannot wait until you finish letting the rest of those cats out of the bag, once and for all." Secretly Bonnie hoped they would not turn out to be cats of the skunk variety!

All three of them scurried about. Mel's dad was somewhat reluctant to believe Mel's claims, but not Mel; he was sure he had done the necessary detective homework. He felt his grandfather's spirit leading him to find more hidden gold coins. The feeling was stronger than ever, and Mel had no choice but to follow his grandfather's lead.

Mel retrieved two flashlights from the hall closet, and the three of them maneuvered their way out of the house and into the car like a well-trained military platoon. They soon pulled into the church parking lot, where they all got out and headed for the church's basement. Mel's dad calmly unlocked the door. Flicking on the light switch at the top of the stairs, they turned on the two flashlights and headed down into the basement. Mel pointed his flashlight across the room in the direction of the b okcase, which had fallen in a heap. It was still blocking the door they had used to enter the church a few days earlier. Both flashlights shined on the pile of books scattered among the big wooden bookshelf. It looked as though an earthquake had toppled the gigantic wooden shelves. Mel pointed his flashlight at the wall against which the bookcase had stood for hundreds of years. There he could see something hanging on the wall. Looking very closely they all could see a small golden crucifix hanging from a hook. Mel, stepping through the bookcase and the toppled books, took the chain with the cross hanging on it and held it under the light of the flashlight. Bonnie, on one side of Mel, and Mel's dad, on his other side, stood looking at the exquisite artifact. It certainly looked to be solid gold, and it had small red stones inset to echo the essences of the blood of Jesus, who was nailed to the priceless cross.

"Son, is this what you were looking for?" Pastor Dread asked, taking the valuable chain and cross from Mel's open hand. "No!" Mel answered.

Mel's dad was confused. "Well then, what were you looking for, Mel?" both little Bonnie and Pastor Dread asked at the very same time.

Mel, taking charge of the situation, commanded that his father go find a big hammer—or better yet, a sledgehammer.

"You have got to be kidding," his father said, disappearing into the basement to look for a sledgehammer of sorts. It was not a very difficult task, as the basement of the church was full of things from the past hundred years.

Standing next to Mel once again, Pastor Dread asked Mel, "Now what, Son?"

Taking the flashlight from his dad, Mel handed it to little Bonnie. "Dad," Mel said, "Bonnie and I will keep the flashlights pointed toward the wall where the crucifix was hanging."

Chuckling, Mel let his dad know that it would give Mel great pleasure to be able to take the first swing at the wall; unfortunately he only had one good arm.

Holding up his broken arm, Mel said, "Please, Father, be my guest. Simply knock a hole in the concrete wall where the gold crucifix was hanging."

Mel's father, for the first time ever in his entire life, did exactly what Mel had asked him to do. Like a younger man half his age, the pastor picked up the sledgehammer. He made a horrible cry, like Tarzan of the jungle, as he swung the heavy sledgehammer, hitting the concrete wall.

Bonk! Pastor Dread lost hold of the sledgehammer, and it ricocheted, almost hitting Mel in the head.

"Whoa," Mel yelled. "Whoa, Dad. Hit the wall just a bit lower." Mel's dad picked up the sledgehammer and wound up for his second swing at the wall. This time, when the hammer hit the wall, there was a sound of the wall breaking up. Pastor Dread, from the horrendous force of the impact, had let go of the sledgehammer.

The sledgehammer was now embedded deep in the wall, stuck in the hole it had made.

"Perfect aim, Dad," Mel was yelling with extreme joy. It was as if Mel had delivered the forceful blow to the wall himself.

"Yes," cried Bonnie. She was excited as any of them were. She was thinking it was lucky for them she had a broken arm because otherwise by now she would have pushed Pastor Dread out of the way to take another swing at the wall herself.

Pastor Dread pulled the sledgehammer out of the wall. Mel handed his father a flashlight. Pastor Dread, holding the flashlight, looked into the hole in the wall. He said, "I am sorry, Son. I do not see a single thing." Taking his hand and cleaning out pieces of cement from the hole, he looked in again and said, "Nope, Son. I see absolutely nothing."

"No!" Mel yelled. "No, I cannot believe it. Something is wrong." Mel had never felt such madness. Maybe it was true, as they had all said: looking for lost treasure could drive you crazy. Picking up a big book in his left hand, Mel slammed it against the wall right above the empty hole his dad had made.

Thinking she had just seen something fall out of the hole in the wall, Bonnie picked up another book and threw it as hard as she could at the hole. They stood there watching as one gold coin fell out of the hole. Then came another and another. The coins began falling out of the hole as if they were in a Las Vegas casino and they had just hit the jackpot! Pastor Dread did not say a word; he just stood there in shock. Mel was astounded at how many gold coins kept falling out the hole.

Little Bonnie, not at all lost for words, was singing, "We're in the money, we're in the money" while jumping up and down. Little Bonnie was so extremely happy that, with her help, Detective Mel Porter Dread IV had finally been able to solve the Dread family mystery. Pastor Dread, quicker than a jackrabbit dodging a bullet, found two five-gallon plastic buckets. With the help of his onehanded comrades, he worked hard to scoop up every one of those gold coins.

After they carefully hid the two buckets of gold coins behind some old boxes piled against a wall, Pastor Dread took a moment to throw some old curtains over the buckets. It was time for them to get out of the church basement, go home, and try to comprehend what had happened that morning.

Mel could not help but think that this would be the turning point in his career as a famous detective. It would not be long before Mel would be turning thirteen, and he was sure that next year would prove to be even more insane then this summer had been! Suddenly Mel was thinking about all the changes that his dad had said were soon to come. What could it be, Mel thought, still fearing some possible wrath from God. Maybe there was a curse connected to finding the Dread family treasure. *Oh my Gawd,* Mel thought, *what have I done? I am too rich to die this young!*

Pastor Dread, taking a hold of little Bonnie's hand, led her out of the church basement as Mel followed. While the three of them were making their way out of the basement, Mel said to his father, "Dad, do you think there could have been some awful curse connected to anyone who found the hidden gold?"

"No, Mel," his dad answered. "That's silly, Melvin. It's not like we have been in an Egyptian tomb, digging up Dread people." Mel's father had finally found the humor in Bonnie's Dread jokes.

Bonnie giggled. Pastor Dread motioned for her to head up the basement stairs first. Mel was close behind her, with Pastor Dread bringing up the rear this time. Mel's dad locked up the metal door that led out of the church's basement and checked it twice. He then ushered Mel and Bonnie out of the church and closed the doors behind him, once again double-checking to make sure that door was also locked securely.

Looking at his watch, Mr. Dread unlocked the car doors. They all got in the car and headed back to the house. Pulling into the driveway, they could see a red car that was parked in their driveway. Someone appeared to be sitting in it, waiting for them to arrive home. Mel said, "Who are you expecting, Dad?"

Mel's dad turned his head to look into Mel's eyes and said, "I wanted to find time to tell you sooner, Son. It's been so hectic, with you and Bonnie both breaking your arms and me following while you two found the lost family treasure. Plus, I did not know how to tell you, Mel. That person waiting in that car is here to see you, Mel. That person is your…"

"Who is it?" Mel quickly interrupted his father. "Do I know who it is, Dad?" Mel asked once more suspiciously.

"It's your mother, Mel."

Looking out the window, Mel could see a tall, slender lady get out of her car. She had beautiful, brown, shoulder-length hair. She wore a light blue blouse and had on tight jeans. She looked a bit like a movie actress standing there, waiting for them to open their car doors.

Walking up to Mel, the lady said, "My, my, my, Melvin P. Dread IV. Child, how you have grown! You certainly have grown into a fine young man. I can't believe how handsome you are. You look so much like all the other Dread men, but I think you have your grandma's big eyes."

"Hello," said Mel's father. It's funny how much things change, yet so much stays the same.

The pretty lady said, "You're looking well, Porter."

Bonnie, not missing a word, said, "Hi. My name's Bonnie Lou Starr." She stuck out her good hand. "It's a pleasure to finally meet Mel's mama."

"Well, sweetie," the lady answered back, "nice to meet you as well." Without any hesitation, the lady said, "My name is Angela, but my friends call me Angel. You sure are a pretty little girl! How did you two manage to break your arms? Bonnie Lou, were you and Melvin involved in some sort of freak accident?"

Pastor Dread, interrupting, said, "There will be plenty of time to answer all the questions that everyone might be having right now. For now, let's all get in the house and get comfortable." Pastor Dread tried his best to usher them through the front door.

Pastor Dread's head was spinning. He still had not found the right time to tell little Bonnie that both of her parents had been suddenly killed in a head-on car collision last Friday night while she and Mel were trapped in the basement of the church. He had gotten a phone call about it late, late on Sunday evening. On the same day, Mel's mom, Angela, had phoned to say that she was coming by to see her son, Melvin.

Bonnie's parents had informed Pastor Dread of their plan to place Bonnie's grandmother in a convalescent home for the elderly while they were there picking up their daughter. The hospital would not release her grandmother until she could go directly to a full-time care facility. Bonnie's grandmother now lost her ability to take care of herself. There seemed to be no other choice for Bonnie's parents than to place her somewhere that offered full-time, around-the-clock care.

"Angel, can I fix you some tea?" Mr. Dread asked.

"Why, that sounds delightful, Mel. Two sugars and a tiny bit of cream, please, Porter. Well, Melvin, what have you been up to this summer? You are such a big boy now. I am sure you are always busy getting into all kinds of trouble!"

Mel answered politely, "Oh, this summer was just another uneventful summer, I mostly hung out, spent time with my friend Bonnie, watched TV, or rode my bike." He smiled at Angela. Mel could not stop staring at the woman who was sitting across from him, the woman who was supposedly his mother. His mother was one of the few things Mel had no memory of. He could not remember her ever being his mom! Mel kept wondering to himself why she had come back here now, because Mel P. Dread certainly did not believe she had much interest in him, her son, no matter what she said!

"The tea is ready, and I hope it is just how you like it." Pastor Dread told Mel and Bonnie that he had set them out some cold sodas and asked Mel if he would go get the drinks from the kitchen counter. "Not at all, Dad. Come on, Bonnie. Let's find something to eat along with our sodas." Both standing up, they marched into the kitchen, out of sight from Mel's dad and his long-lost mother, Angela. "This is all just too much to comprehend," Mel said to little Bonnie. "I cannot believe that of all the days someone's long-lost mother could return, she would pics the same day her estranged son solved the last remaining mystery of the Dread family treasure." Little Bonnie was at a loss of what to say, so she just listened. Mel for the fir t time saw the world differently. It was not about being rich or being poor; it was about being in control. It did not matter how far one was down the pecking order. Unless you were the head chicken, you had little control over your destiny. Mel knew that once his life had seemed much simpler, maybe because he was living with his grandfather and doing mostly as he wanted to. Now, suddenly, he felt trapped, like a cat in a bag. Mel felt like running, but he had no idea where. Then he heard his grandfather's words, "Never run if you can stand and fight your battles!"

"Bonnie," Mel said, "I fear the worst is yet to come. So, my dear little Bonnie, no matter what happens to either of us, we have to find a way to stay together." Looking at her, he said, "You're the only friend I have ever had, Bonnie Lou Starr. I would give all the treasure we found back to the church if I could just always have you as my best friend."

"Hey kids," called a voice from the living room, "did you two fall down again and break your other arms?" The sounds of laughing came from the living room. They returned to where Pastor Dread and Angela sat talking.

"So," Mel said, looking at his mother, "I cannot help but wonder how long you are here for."

"I must be leaving shortly, Melvin," she answered. "I just wanted to stop in after all these years and tell you how sorry I am not to have kept in touch with you, Son. Someday I hope I will have the opportunity to explain why I left you as a baby so long ago. But right now is not the time for that conversation. Things will change soon if you will forgive me and let me be a part of your life again, Mel."

Mel, not knowing what to say, said, "Oh, swell. That would be really swell." Excusing himself, he went to the bathroom, put his head in the toilet, and threw up!

Mel, reappearing, could see that everyone was on their feet. Mel could see Angela, his mother, saying good-bye to little Bonnie as well as to his father.

"Come here, Melvin P. Dread IV. Give Angel a big hug. I will be keeping in touch, Son," she proclaimed loudly. Mel stood there in a foggy haze, as Angel hugged him, gave him a big kiss, and walked out the front door. It was very dark out, and you could see her car lights turn on as she ba ked out of the driveway.

"Well," Pastor Dread said to Mel and Bonnie, who were standing there with their arms in slings, "that, my son, was your mother. I hope her stopping to visit has not upset you, Son. Your mother knows she has missed out on getting to participate in your life for the last eight years, Mel, and she is truly interested in the two of you getting to know one another again."

To Mel it was of little consequence what this woman who gave him birth wanted. Mel saw her as an unwanted intruder who seemed to think that somehow she could just walk right back into his life because she felt as if she had missed something. Mel thought, *I got along without her before I met her, and I am going to get along without you now, boom boom, boom boom, going to get along without you now.* It was one of many old songs that Mel's grandfather had taught him to sing before he died.

Mel pulled back the curtains and watched his mother drive down the street out of sight.

It was almost 9:00 p.m. when they finished eating dinner and washed up the dishes. Everything was definitely a much slower process with both Bonnie's and Mel's arms in heavy plaster casts. Finishing in the kitchen, Bonnie wandered upstairs. Mel found his father in the study. His father had his eyes closed. He was clinging to his Bible and praying deeply. Mel stood there quietly. When his father finally opened his eyes, Mel said, "Dad, I don't understand where all these premonitions that I continually seem to have come from. I feel like all hell is going to break loose any moment, so if you could, would you explain to me what you meant when you said there were going to be a lot of changes that would be affecting all of us? I need you to shoot straight with me, Dad. What in the heck is going on?"

Pastor Dread said, "Sit down, Son. I am not sure where to begin. First, Mel, please be assured that no matter what life throws our way, we must always remember that God is there to help us through the good times as well as the terrible times."

"Dad," Mel said, "today I found grandfather's treasure. The same day my mother, who has be n gone most of my life, shows up. Please tell me what else this day is going to reveal to me. What have you not told me, Dad? What did you mean when you said, 'Help us through these terrible times?' What terrible times, Dad?" "Mel, there is no easy way to tell you this, but little Bonnie's parents were killed in a head-on collision this past Friday night while on their way here to Ainsworth. They planned to put Bonnie's grandmother in a convalescent center and drive little Bonnie back home to Nebraska so she could get ready for the new school year." Pastor Dread confessed to Mel that he had not yet found the right time or had the heart to tell little Bonnie Lou Starr that both her mother and her father were now deceased and with God. It was breaking his heart to have to tell her.

Mel, in a state of shock said, "Dad, please let me tell her. She is my best friend, and we have been through so very much together already. I feel like it is my responsibility and my job to look after little Bonnie, especially now, when she has no other family but us."

CHAPTER 12

Best of Friends Forever or Sometimes the End Is Just the Beginning

Mel, not knowing what to say to his best friend, marched up the stairs and down the hall to the bedroom where little Bonnie was in her pajamas, lying on her bed.

"Bonnie," Mel asked, "are you still awake?"

Bonnie answered, "Yes, Mel. I cannot fall asleep. I am too worried about my mom and my dad. I have not heard from them in a few days now. That's not uncommon," she added, "except they should have been here today to see my grandmother and me."

Mel sat down next to little Bonnie on her bed. "Bonnie," Mel said, "what if I told you that from now on you were going to live here with my dad and me, and when your grandmother is well enough, she can come live with us too. What do you think of that plan, Missy?" Mel asked.

Little Bonnie, sitting up and looking deep into Mel's eyes, said, "That would be a splendid thought, Melvin P. Dread, wouldn't it?"

Mel began to cry.

"Mel, what's wrong?" Bonnie was upset to see Mel crying. She reached over and gave him a hug. Mel hugged little Bonnie back. As they wrapped their arms around each other, Mel whispered into Bonnie's left ear, "Your mom and dad were killed in a car crash two days ago. I am so sorry!"

Where does your mind go when you are suddenly confronted with the mortality of your mother and your father? Where do you find the understanding at twelve years old to comprehend the travesty that takes place every day on our streets and highways? Now the children were forced to realize that accidents don't just happen to other people's loved ones.

The next week was the last week of Mel and Bonnie's summer vacation. Bonnie and Mel had their share of crying that week. Bonnie struggled to comprehend that her dad and her mom were forever gone, gone to where everyone goes after they die. She was hoping they were both in heaven.

Mel and little Bonnie spent many hours together in the hammock, laughing, crying, and swinging gently back and forth in the warm fall air. They also planned how to spend those six gold coins, knowing when they reached their eighteenth birthday the rest of the treasure would be theirs to do with as they pleased. Until that day, Pastor Dread would remain guardian of the Dread family treasure. As for the priceless gold crucifix that had been found hanging on the copper hook behind the bookcase, Pastor Dread had decided for now that he would keep the gold crucifix in his possession. No one but him would have to know. Mel's dad took great measures to carefully hide the crucifix where no one would ever possibly find it except him.

All the arrangements had be n made. Next week Bonnie was enrolled to start seventh grade. Mel and Bonnie would have the same homeroom, which could not be more awesome.

Little Bonnie's grandmother would soon be moving into the Dread family's fourth bedroom. It was on the first floor, next to Pastor Dread's bedroom Little Bonnie could not wait to help take care of her grandmother, who she was sure would make a complete recovery.

Angela, Mel's mom, sent a big box of new school clothes for both Mel and Bonnie to wear. It was Angela's way to let them both know that she wanted them all back in her life—and that included Mel's father, Melvin P. Dread III. As the former Mrs. Melvin Porter Dread realized, it would not happen overnight, but Angela was just like her son. She did not easily give up on what she was hoping to find! So Mel's mom would start to show up more and more as fall turned into winter once again. There were so many questions and so many answers. Some questions had no answers, like did God really love the poor as much as he loved the rich? To Mel it was a question of how God defined love. Maybe it had little to do with money and more to do with the pure acts of kindness. As they lay in that hammock those last few days of summer, Bonnie's and Mel's broken arms were still encased in their white casts. One cast was signed, "To the best assistant any detective ever had, from Melvin Porter Dread, your best friend always." Little Bonnie had written on Mel's cast, "Show me the money," referring to those priceless six gold coins that only she and Mel knew about, which would come in handy to buy all kinds of stuff, from purple cell phones to healthier junk food. Life was good, in spite of it all.

After all, it was what it was.

Soon Mel and Bonnie were heading off to Clyde's Gold for Cash Shop, where Mel was prepared to sell one of the six gold coins for much more than the five hundred dollars he had been offered before by Darrell. Bonnie did not care how much they got. She was just happy to know that half of whatever it was would be hers to spend. Pedaling her bike alongside her best friend, little Bonnie happily sang, "I'm in the money, Mel's in the money, we're in the money."

Mel and Bonnie were both feeling the love from God above.

It was a priceless feeling. It felt as though they just might be the richest kids in the whole wide world in so many ways.

They had no doubt that God did love both of them, the two once poor kids from rural Nebraska.

About the Author

The Mel P. Dread mystery series describes the adventures of two seventh-grade kids brought together during their summer vacation in a small town in rural Nebraska.

The author, John P. Kaufman, grew up on a rural dairy farm in Michigan. He was one of seven brothers and sisters. He has worked as a classroom teacher and educator. He studied history and art at Eastern Michigan University, where he earned his bachelor's degree in art education.

After working on his master's at Michigan State University, in 1980 he moved to Tucson, Arizona, where he will tell you he loves the dry heat of the desert. His favorite things are writing, painting, art, travel, and keeping fit, and he is always happy to be active while working on a multitude of his inventive ideas and other creative projects.

Currently the author is working on his second Mel Porter Dread mystery. The book entitled, *You're Not Dead until Someone Finds Your Corpse*, starts out in a movie theater where we can hear the sounds of blood curdling screams! This time Mel and his best friend Bonnie Starr find themselves entangled knee deep in a canine crime scene involving dogs, diamonds, and the Russian mafia.

There is nothing better than a good mystery!